LAST STOP ON THE TRAIL

When Eli Grant and his gang hit town they stirred up a hornet's nest that got Eli's brother a bullet in the heart and space in Boot Hill. Then they made another mistake. They came back for revenge which set Sheriff Jack Holland on their trail. But Jack had his own problems with the posse and another set of outlaws. Treachery was in the offing and many men would die before peace came to the town.

H. H. CODY

LAST STOP ON THE TRAIL

Complete and Unabridged

LINFORD
Leicester

First published in Great Britain in 1996 by
Robert Hale Limited
London

First Linford Edition
published 1997
by arrangement with
Robert Hale Limited
London

British Library CIP Data

Cod, H. H.
Last stop on the trail.—Large print ed.—
Linford western library
1. Western stories
2. Large type books
I. Title
823.9′14 [F]

ISBN 0–7089–5148–1

Published by
F. A. Thorpe (Publishing) Ltd.
Anstey, Leicestershire

Set by Words & Graphics Ltd.
Anstey, Leicestershire
Printed and bound in Great Britain by
T. J. International Ltd., Padstow, Cornwall

This book is printed on acid-free paper

1

THERE were four of them: tired, hungry, running men who had ridden down through Arizona leaving a dozen shot-up banks and plundered stages in their bloody wake. Men whose faces had appeared on dodger posters all over the state. Men who could feel the rope tightening around their necks, waiting for the snap of the lever and the trapdoor to fall open, the short drop, and the jerk of the rope that would send them to hell. Men who had ridden with 'Bloody' Bill Anderson during the War between the States. Men who had ridden into Centralia, Missouri, in autumn 1863, sacked the town, stopped a train and took $3,000 off it then murdered the bluebellies going home on furlough.

With the ending of the war, when every sensible, law-abiding man had gone home, they'd taken the outlaw trail, leaving blood and misery wherever they went.

Now, they were headed for the safety of the Mexican border and the sanctuary it offered. They had crossed the Colorado and given Yuma a superstitiously wide berth and splashed through the Gila. But there was one more town to hit, a debt to be paid. Red Bluff.

Eli Gant's small, yellow eyes peered deeply into the flames of the camp-fire, still seeing his brother, Mordecai, who had survived the war only to be killed falling from the saddle by a Yankee sheriff. Even now, twelve months after the sheriff of Red Bluff, Jack Holland, had nearly finished Eli's career as an outlaw and murderer forever, and sure as hell finished Mordecai's, he still felt the pain where the slug from Holland's .45 had ripped into his arm.

Holland had shot his brother out of the saddle as they hightailed it down Main Street with almost everybody in the town doing their damnedest to plug them. Bad luck had ridden with them that day; they had chosen to hit the bank on the day that a small consignment of silver had been delivered to the same bank escorted by a dozen men.

Gant could still see the sheriff stepping off the porch into the dusty street to line up Mordecai in the sights of his six gun. He could still see the hot sun reflected by the tin star on the sheriff's vest, the flash of flame, then the scream of Mordecai as he flung out his arms and hit the dust.

Quickly, Gant had thrown a shot at the sheriff but missed. Turning, as they galloped by, he saw Holland firing at him, then felt the burning pain in his shoulder. It had been all that Gant could do to stay in the saddle, but he had done it and, seconds later, they were on the outskirts of Red Bluff, empty handed with the silver escort riding hard after them.

The escort had dogged them day and

night. Gant had lost two of his gang but, finally, they managed to shake off their pursuers. Then they had headed north, where the pickings were easier than in the south.

Gant picked up his fork and plate of beans. Forking the beans into his mouth, he turned to see the baby-faced killer, Morley, sitting propped against the cave wall, a plate in his hand, his carbine by his side, crossed ammunition belts over his chest.

"Git down the trail an' send Dak in for some coffee an' chow," he said, through the mash of food in his mouth.

Grumbling something about the cold, Morley got to his feet and, picking up his carbine, ducked low out of the cave. He kept close to the wall of rocks until he found Dak, peering over some boulders watching the trail. Dak swung sharply, his pistol in his hand when Morley's foot hit a stone. Nobody knew his other name. They just called the burly, bearded man Dak. Once in a town in Texas, Morley had heard a man ask him his Christian name, if Christian he was, which Morley doubted; Dak had not replied and, when the man repeated his question, Dak pulled his double-bladed knife and cut off the man's earlobe. He was the knifeman of the outfit. He could skin a dog or a man in no time at all. And he liked doing it. A true artist, Morley thought.

"Fella could git killed," Dak said tiredly, shoving the .46 into its holster, sneakin' about like that."

"Fella could git killed anyway if these Apaches git wind of us." Morley hunkered down beside Dak. "See anythin'?"

"Nary a thing." Rummaging inside his coat Dak hauled out a bottle of whiskey. "Here, don't drink it all."

"Thanks, pard." Morley bit out the cork. Dropping it into his hand he tilted the bottle to his lips and drank greedily. The warmth sure felt good, he told himself.

Shoving the cork back in, he put the bottle on a ledge, got his carbine and pushed it up beside the bottle.

The thought of the saddle-bag that contained the gang's accumulated wealth being out of his sight bothered him considerably. When Gant had first told them of his intention to teach Red Bluff a lesson, Morley felt in his bones that it was all wrong. Going back for a second bite at the cherry was bad news, especially a prickly cherry like Red Bluff. It was tough on Mordecai, but those who took the outlaw trail knew the risks.

He could remember the nights and days on the trail when he thought he was going to decorate a tree somewhere or a newly built scaffold in Red Bluff, and he wanted no part of that. No, he had other plans. And those plans didn't include Eli, Dak or Wicks. No, sir, not at all. They included a pretty little piece of baggage by the name of Belle. Belle was the finest whore Morley had ever paid good money to be with for many a day or night. Not only was she good at her job, but she was pretty to boot. When he had the saddle-bag and Belle, they were heading for South America to open a cat house. He settled himself to wait the night out.

Gant woke first. He felt good. Today he was going to settle with Red Bluff and Jack Holland. He kicked Wicks awake. Cold and stiff, the man got to his feet.

"Git that fire goin'. Might as well have some grub inside us 'fore we go."

Leaving Wicks to rouse Dak, he went out to find Morley. Though the day had only just started, the temperature was already climbing. Sweat ran down Gant's face, making a trail through the dust; it plastered the shirt to his back and stuck his hatband to his greasy black hair.

Without a word Morley handed Gant the bottle and watched him drink from it. Coughing and spluttering, Gant wiped his mouth on the sleeve of his buckskin jacket.

Then he said, "Anythin' movin'?"

Morley shook his head as he cut himself a hunk of chewing tobacco.

"Let's get some chow." Gant led the way back to the camp. Finding enough wood to get a fire started Wicks hunkered over it, his thin face alive at the prospect of shooting up Red Bluff. He'd ridden with them the last time they hit the place and, like the others, had an urge to get back there and settle things.

Wicks had got the fire going and was warming up the coffee and beans from last night. They ate in silence standing deep in the cooling shadow of the cave, tearing the last hunk of stale bread into pieces and sharing it out.

When he had finished Gant kicked dust over the fire.

"All right." Gant had broken open his .46 to check the loads. The others did the same.

"Let's ride," he snapped.

They mounted up and cantered out into the desert.

2

RED BLUFF was a no-account kind of town, that is to anybody who didn't live there. Those who did live there liked it. They brought up their children, sent them to the school just outside town past the newly built church. The cowboys who came in on Saturday night to spend their pay stayed at the opposite end of town where the cat house stood along with the two saloons, The Drover's Rest and the Prairie Rose.

Jack Holland's office stood roughly half–way down Main Street. There were only a couple of other streets running off it. One of them housed a second general store, which the mayor said was a sign of the town's growing prosperity, and there was a café and a barber's. The town had started to grow once people realized that it was not going to be another boom town when the silver the old miner had found turned out to be just one vein. This settled people. There would be no drifters, gunmen or gamblers. The town had started to settle down before it got out of hand and the firmness of Jack Holland made sure it stayed settled down.

Standing on the step of his office, Jack Holland figured that there was trouble by the way Slim Carney's horse tore up the dust as it came in his direction. Carney rode for the Circle K, whose land stretched from the river to the county boundary two miles out of town. Holland hoped it wasn't serious. His wife, Claire, was coming in from their house out beyond the church to do some shopping. Holland had promised to help her get it back to the house.

Carney dragged the horse to a halt outside the office, sweat running down his beefy, red face. He ran up the steps to where Holland waited for him.

"Take it easy, Slim, or you're gonna melt in this heat," Holland laughed.

"Had a shooting at the ranch," Slim gasped out, running his bandanna over his face.

"Best come inside where it's cooler an' tell me about it." Holland led him into the small office. Pointing to a swivel chair he indicated for Slim to sit down.

"Now, what's this all about?" Holland asked.

"Ol' Jasper got likkered up last night, an' picked a fight with Ben Travis. Travis shot him." Carney had flopped in the chair, the underarms of his shirt black with sweat.

"Anybody killed?" Holland reached for a pencil and used the back of a dodger poster to write down the details.

"Uh — uh," snorted Carney, fanning himself with his stetson. "Ike Slattery says can you come over and sort it out?"

The promise of helping Claire with the shopping and having a meal at

Marquita's melted like a mirage before Holland's eyes.

"Don't see why not, that's why I'm here." Hastily he wrote a note to his deputy and got up.

"Come on, Slim. Time's a'wastin'," he said heading for the door. He went outside, grinning as Slim Carney hauled his bulk out of the swivel chair and followed him.

"We got time for me to wet my whistle?" Carney asked. "It's been a wicked ride." He turned in the direction of the Prairie Rose.

"Guess so." Holland stuck the note for his deputy on a nail by the side of the door. "Besides, I've got to go down to the livery for my horse. Just one," he added knowing Slim's capacity for beer, lukewarm or otherwise.

"Thanks Jack," the fat rider said, ambling off in the direction of the saloon.

"And make sure your horse gets some water as well," Holland called after him.

Heading for the livery at the other end of town, Holland pulled at the back of his shirt which had started to stick to his back.

"Mornin', Jack," Sam Kilbourne called out from the shade of his awning outside his blacksmith's.

"Hi, Sam," Holland called back, watching the flames in the grate. Kilbourne had a horseshoe held by a pair of tongs and was hammering away at it. Holland did not envy the man his task in this heat. The sweat shone on Kilbourne's muscular body. A couple of times he stopped hammering to wipe the sweat out of his eyes.

Holland thought that as bad as the ride out to the ranch would be, it sure as hell was better than standing hammering in front of a fire all day. As he got to the livery, Pettifer, the owner came out, like everybody else sweating like a pig, water running down his face and dropping off his weak chin.

"G'day, Sheriff," he sang out effusively. Pettifer was a small man with an ingratiating attitude, a weak face and a sloping jaw.

"Mornin'. Can you saddle up my horse, Miles?" Holland watched Pettifer disappear into the livery stable. Holland waited in the shadow of the tree that stood outside the livery until Pettifer came out again leading his big bay.

"Somebody got trouble?" Pettifer enquired, rubbing his hands against his soiled apron.

"Can't tell 'til I get there." Holland never liked telling people more than he had to. Taking the bay's leathers he led her back to the jail, passing Marquita's café. Through the window he could see Saul McBean, his deputy, laying into a big breakfast.

"'Bout time you were making an honest woman of the widow Elam," Holland muttered to himself as he passed the café.

When he got to the jail Carney's horse had gone.

"Hey," called out Holland, to a passing youngster. He took the note down from the nail beside the door. "Take this down to Marquita's place. Give it to my deputy."

"Sure will, Sheriff." The boy took the paper and scooted off. A few moments later Carney and his horse appeared looking refreshed from their respective drinks.

"Let's get going." Holland pushed a booted foot into the stirrup and hauled himself into the saddle. Both men took it easy leaving town, when they got out on to the trail they speeded up a mite.

An hour later they came upon the first cattle of the Circle K, a few scraggy head mooching in the sparse, dry grass, trying to get a good mouthful. A cowboy, whose name Holland did not know, threw them a greeting.

"Travis's in the barn; got it all forted up. Best watch your head, Sheriff," he called out as they passed him by.

"Damn it," swore Carney. "Musta got loose. Had him hog-tied in the bunkhouse when I came lookin' for you."

"It doesn't master," Holland told him. "I'll get him out. Travis ain't a bad sort of cuss. Except when he gets some drink down him."

"Ain't that the truth," scowled Carney as they sweated. The day wasn't getting any cooler.

About the time that Holland and the cowboy exchanged greetings a buckboard was drawing up outside one of Red Bluff's general stores. Claire Holland climbed down from the platform. Saul McBean, with his boss's note in his hand stepped forward to greet her.

"Mornin', Claire," he said affably. "You're looking pretty this morning."

"Why thank you, kind sir," Claire retorted with a mock curtsey.

She and Saul were old friends since before the time that Jack Holland had drifted into town after the war. Jack had stayed to marry Claire and become sheriff. There had been those who had said that it would lead to trouble between the two men. Holland, a johnny-cum-lately, had married the most beautiful woman in the territory and Saul McBean had been hotly tipped to take her down the aisle. But there hadn't been any trouble; Saul had no ambition in Claire's direction, and was content to settle for being deputy.

"Got a message from Jack. He's had to go out to the Circle K. Don't know when he'll be back."

A frown of irritation crossed Claire Holland's face. She and Jack didn't get to spend too much time to do anything together.

"Just to make it up, suppose I buy you coffee and a piece of pie at Marquita's?" Saul offered gallantly.

For a moment Claire thought about his offer.

"That's very nice of you. I've got to go to the bank for some extra cash. I'll see you at Marquita's in about fifteen minutes," she said.

"Fifteen minutes," Saul replied, watching four men ride slowly into town.

3

THE four men had ridden in silence. Now, they were outside Red Bluff, perched on the edge of the trail like four hungry vultures waiting for a sick animal to die. The town seemed asleep under the blistering heat of the sun. Gant sleeved the sweat from his eyes to get a better view. The others waited expectantly, the horses nervously pawing the ground.

"Don't seem too much activity," Morley said, as he licked his dry lips. "Leastways there won't be any gunnies from the silver company waiting for us this time."

"Sure ain't," Gant replied, his mean eyes taking it all in. "An' are they gonna be sorry." He gave a dry laugh.

Rowelling his horse, he urged it forward. "Come on."

They passed the school with the

children playing and shouting noisily despite the heat. As the outlaws passed, a hush seemed to come over the youngsters, as though they sensed the evil in the air. On the step of the church the preacher, a thin, nervous German, stopped then went back inside.

Main Street stood virtually empty, the buildings shimmering, the wood drying and cracking. As they approached the bank a slim woman was heading that way. Dak nudged Wicks and pointed to her, giving an obscene leer.

"Ain't gonna be time for that," Gant hissed, watching her go to the bank.

"Real pity," Morley opined, rubbing his crotch. "Could do a woman with a body like that a power of good."

For a moment or two they halted at the intersection of two streets, giving one last gander up and down before they struck.

"Dak, you hold the horses; start shooting if anybody gits nosy." They rode across the street, dismounted and handed the leathers up to him.

Inside the bank Claire Holland smiled a greeting to the two tellers behind their cages.

Harold Smalltop had hired Bernard Garland as junior teller in the Red Bluff because James Downham was due to retire at the end of the week.

Bernard had just taken Claire's withdrawal slip from her when Gant came in. At first he did not see the .46 in the outlaw's hand, thinking that he was just another customer. He had handed Claire her money when Morley and Wicks followed him in. Their unshaven evil faces caused him to take another look at Gant.

Claire saw the colour drain from his face as his hands went up. She turned slowly and saw the reason why and gave a little gasp. The bank's chief teller, the elderly James Downham, was standing next to Bernard; he too saw the gun and raised his hands.

"Keep them hands where we can see them. That goes for you as well, sweetheart," Gant rasped out, his yellow eyes running over Claire's body.

"Your boss in?" Gant took a step up to Garland's cage, waggling his gun through the bars and nodding towards the door.

Garland nodded nervously, his eyes never leaving Gant's pistol.

"Shout him in here," Gant said, looking at the manager's door.

"Mr Smalltop," Garland called out in a dry voice, "could you come out here please?"

He waited. There was no reply. Gant gestured impatiently with the gun. Garland shouted again. This time from the manager's office came the scrape of a chair being pushed away from a desk, then the heavy clump of boots. A second later the door opened and Harold Smalltop appeared at the door, his face red with anger at being disturbed. He had been writing a little speech to deliver to James Downham at the surprise party that had been planned for him on Friday afternoon when the bank had closed.

His mouth opened to make some irritable comment to Garland when he saw the outlaws. His face paled; the fleshy jaws quivered in fear.

"Git 'em up, fat boy," Morley ordered with a chilling laugh.

"What do you want?" Smalltop enquired nervously, his jowls shaking as he spoke.

Gant echoed Morley's laugh. "Your bank's money, what d'you think?"

"Er — er, yes." Smalltop's voice quaked with his fear.

Pulling a couple of bags from his coat, Gant tossed them across to him. Passing the bags to Downham, Smalltop told him to hurry, the sooner the three men were off the premises the better he would feel. His fingers sticking to the bills Downham worked as fast as he could, worrying that another customer would walk in and startle the outlaws into shooting.

"Come on, git a move on," Wicks said, pushing the curtain aside so that he could get a look out into the street. The only person he could see out there was Dak holding the leathers of the horses.

Thrusting the last of the bills into the bag, he was about to toss it to Gant, when Gant spotted the greenbacks in Claire's hand.

"Them too." He pointed at the bundle.

Claire turned quickly to look at Downham, then back to Gant.

"No," she said, shakily, but with a trace of defiance in her voice; her hand closed more tightly around the bills.

"Hurry up, you stupid bitch," Gant snarled, taking a threatening step forward, the gun coming up level with her midriff.

"Do as he says, Mrs Holland," Downham put in.

Gant's head came round sharply. "Holland? You the sheriff's wife?"

Before she could think clearly, Claire said, "The sheriff is my husband."

Downham watched as an expression

of pure hatred crossed Gant's ugly face. The others looked at her.

"Morley," Gant said as he holstered his pistol, "see anybody out there?"

"Only Dak; want I should git him in here?" Morley asked, pushing the curtain back with the barrel of his gun.

"Ain't time. Dak's gonna miss the fun, but we'll make it up to him." Reaching out, suddenly Gant tore Claire's dress from her body. As she screamed he slapped her across the face, a blow that sent her staggering back against the counter.

"Hold her, Wicks," Gant rasped out as he slapped her again. A hand print in deep red appeared on the terrified woman's face as the tears welled in her eyes. As Wicks dragged her to the floor Morley caught sight of a gold cross on a gold chain dangling from Claire's throat. Swiftly he tore it off and put it in his pocket.

Knowing what they were going to do, James Downham could not bear to see it happen to his friend's wife. He reached under the counter to where he kept a pistol. As he dragged it out, Morley saw him. The single shot from Morley blasted into his head, spinning him back against the wall.

"Hell," swore Gant. Swiftly, he turned to where Bernard Garland stood. Bernard's mouth hung open. Gant shot him between the eyes. Smalltop went to run back into his office and slam the door. Wicks' bullet struck him between the shoulder-blades.

"Ain't gonna have that fun with you after all, Mrs Holland." Gant gave a twisted sneer. Slowly, he put the gun to Claire's head and shot her. Within minutes of them coming into the bank the outlaws had turned it into a slaughterhouse.

Nobody appeared to have heard the first shot. McBean went on waiting for Claire Holland in Marquita's. Kilbourne went on fixing up the horseshoes; Pettifer kept on sweeping out his livery stable. The second shot registered, and by the time Gant killed Claire Holland, folks were reaching for their guns.

McBean pushed through the crowd of customers clogging up the doorway out of the café, his gun in his hand, the hammer back. Carefully, keeping under the veranda for cover, he walked in the direction of the bank as Gant came piling out with the others at his heels. Dak aimed his pistol at McBean and fired, but his horse bucked and the slug went high into the wood above McBean's head.

Returning the shot, McBean saw it pluck at the outlaw's hat as his horse bucked once more. Gant and Morley scrambled into their saddles as more slugs came their way. Wicks caught his leathers as the animal reared, frightened by the gunfire and confusion around him. Wicks made it into the saddle just in time for McBean to put a slug high into his chest.

"Bastard's done for me," screamed Wicks, his knuckles gripping the saddle horn, his shirt front reddening with his blood.

"Then I'll do for him," Gant roared back, levelling his pistol at McBean. The slug tore into McBean's heart; he lurched into the street, dead before he hit the dusty ground.

"Let's git outa this hornet's nest," shouted Dak above the noise of the bellowing horses, screaming townsfolk and gunfire.

Aiming their horses down the street they tore off throwing shots in every direction.

4

A TIRED and weary Jack Holland rode back along the trail to Red Bluff. He had managed to sort out the trouble at the Circle K with both men swearing that the whole thing had been a misunderstanding. It was obvious that neither wanted to get the other into any kind of trouble, despite nearly being killed. Before he rode away he had a quiet word with them, warning them of the future consequences if they repeated their actions. Ike Slattery had told them in no uncertain terms that they would be trying to find work elsewhere if they did it again.

His back was aching from the long ride. His clothes plastered to his body and dust blocking every pore, he rounded the bend that would bring Red Bluff into sight. The thought of a warm tub followed by some of Claire's cooking seemed to ease the aches in his body.

The feeling of relief did not last long; as the town came into view he saw a rider approaching him at a fair lick. Holland brought his horse to a standstill in the middle of the trail. At first he could not make out who the approaching rider was because of the dust the horse was throwing up but, from the way he rode his horse, he had trouble. As the rider got nearer and started to slow his horse, Holland recognized him as Gareth Muldoon, son of the editor of the *Red Bluff News*. His horse skidded to a halt within inches of Holland's mount, then stood snorting and heaving for breath. The youth's face was beetroot red, his breath came in great gasps.

"Thank God I found you, Sheriff," Gareth Muldoon said as soon as he got his breath back.

"What's the matter?" demanded Holland, sensing that something really bad had happened.

"Best let Mayor Grossman tell you," Muldoon replied, warily.

Reaching across, Holland put his hand on Muldoon's arm. Muldoon shrugged it off; a look of fear came into his eyes.

"Let Mayor Grossman tell you," he yelled. With that he headed his horse back to town and raced off before Holland could stop him.

Watching him go Holland wondered what had got into the young man. Normally, Gareth Muldoon was polite and friendly, so what had happened in Red Bluff in the last few hours had to be damned serious. Despite the bay's tiredness Holland spared it nothing in his dash to get back to town and learn what had occurred.

A few people were standing on the street corners watching him ride down the street to his office, shaking their heads. He dismounted and tied his horse to the hitch rail and, before going inside, watched the street for a few moments.

More like a Sunday than a week day, he said to himself. Then he went into his office. Franz Grossman, the mayor, stood with his back to Jack Holland's desk.

"What is it, Franz?" Holland tossed his stetson on to the desk and sat down.

Haltingly, Franz Grossman related the morning's events, watching Holland as he did so. He could see sadness then rage form on the sheriff's face.

"Where is she?" Holland asked, getting hold of himself. "I'd like to see her."

"Of course," Franz Grossman replied. "They're in the church."

Holland did not remember the walk from the jail to the church or the pitying glances of the people on the streets. All he could remember was the cool, dark building and the line of coffins on trestles before the altar.

For a moment he stopped before each one, spending a little longer over those of Claire and Saul. When he got outside he apologized to Franz for the way he had spoken to him.

"It doesn't matter, my friend," Franz answered with a choke in his voice. "We will go back to the jail and you can make arrangements for Claire's funeral."

Holland straightened up. "You make the arrangements, old friend. I'll get a posse organized. Don't want Gant getting too much of a head start on us."

Franz had been about to say something when he saw the look in Jack Holland's face. He changed his mind.

When they left the church they separated; Franz went over to the undertaker's, Jack went down to the jail to get a posse organized.

Evidently word had not been slow getting around that he was back; as he approached the jail he saw a number of men in front of it, some carrying rifles and shot-guns. The sight heartened him.

"Sorry to hear about your loss, Jack,"

Kilbourne said. "The sooner we get going the sooner Gant an' his boys will be decorating the woodwork around here."

The crowd growled its agreement.

"Saul got one of them. That ought to slow them down a mite," Kilbourne went on, fingering the stock of the rifle he was carrying.

While they had been talking he had counted them. Ten. Not many, he thought, to go against a bunch of Gant's kind. And most of them married. He hoped they'd catch up with Gant and his gang before the married men in the posse remembered they were married.

For a moment he thought, then said, "Go and get your horses. We'll make a start now. Spend the night at Black Butte, if we ain't caught up with them."

As he watched them disperse he called out to Buck Davies, a half-breed tracker who could be relied on to follow the Devil to Hell, if he had to.

"Buck," he called out. The man

turned, a smile on his face.

"Yes, Jack," he said, his hand resting on the hilt of a hunting knife that hung in his belt.

"What do you reckon to Black Butte?" he said.

"It's the way they were heading. Took my horse out a couple of miles. They were definitely heading for Black Butte," Davies told him.

"Thanks, Buck. Call in at the general store and get some trail grub. Feelin' this might be a long one. And be sure to tell Brocklesby the town'll pay."

"Sure thing," Buck replied, heading for the store.

In the office Holland got down a shot-gun from the wall-rack, his face hard and grim. He broke it open then rooted in the drawer for a box of shells. He loaded the shot-gun with two shells, then put another handful in his jeans pockets. There were other things to check; his pistol; that each loop of his shell-belt held a slug. Going back to the drawer he found a spare pair of cuffs and put them across his belt, the key in his vest pocket.

From the other side of the door he could hear horses and men gathering. Outside he saw that they were ready, ten of them, each one armed. Buck Davies sat on his palomino, a bag slung over his saddle. Brocklesby sat a horse as well, a rifle held across his saddle bow. Alongside him was the blacksmith, Kilbourne, all dressed up in his Sunday best, his face deep red, like the flames he had been tending that morning. To Holland's surprise, he saw Pettifer behind them both, an unfamiliar gun slung across his belly.

"Ready when you are, Jack," Kilbourne called out eagerly, waving his derby in the air. Holland was not going to spend any time arguing or sending him back for something more appropriate to wear.

"All right. Just listen. We're gonna track just as far as Black Butte today, see how we hold up. I know some of you ain't used to hard riding. Besides, they've got a wounded man, so that means they can't get far either."

Feeling that he had said enough Holland swung into the saddle and led them out into the desert towards Black Butte. Evening had started to set in as they rode, a cool breeze fanning them as they went.

5

THE stain on Wicks's chest had spread with great speed. Gant had stopped the headlong rush by his men in order, he said, to give Wicks a breather. Gant positioned himself on a low hill to get a better view of the surrounding country. He figured it would take Holland a couple of hours to get up a posse and start after them.

Dak and Morley had got Wicks out of the saddle and were holding a whiskey bottle to his lips. Wicks's Adam's apple kept going up and down as the level of the whiskey in the bottle went down. Eventually, Morley came up to Gant with the bottle in his hand. Gant took it from him before he could change his mind and finish it himself.

Taking a long swig Gant eyed Morley. "How is he?" he asked,

nodding to Wicks.

"Pretty bad. He's gonna have to have some rest or he's gonna be spillin' his guts all night." Morley took the bottle from Gant and finished it with one swallow.

He flung the bottle into some stunted grass.

"Why don't you just wait for 'em an' save 'em lookin'?" Gant blazed out at him. He went to get the bottle.

"This ground's gonna be no help to their tracker, even if it's Davies, like last time. There ain't no point in leavin' stuff around to make it easy for him. Git it in your saddle-bag." He slapped the bottle into Morley's hands. They walked back, Morley sour-faced, to where the others were waiting. Dak watched them. That Morley was pushing his luck, he thought. Never had his eyes off that saddle-bag since Gant had got all the stuff together and put it in one place. Sometime now Morley was gonna snatch it and run. But it was a cinch where he'd head; straight down to Casa Blanca, the white whorehouse just this side of the border, to that whore he'd met up with.

Dak fingered the bone hilt of his knife. Sure would like to get my hands on that hot little bitch, he thought, and make her squirm.

Gant hunkered down beside Wicks. "Gonna have to be movin' on in a minute. We've spelled the horses, and the posse can't be that far behind."

"I can ride, boss," babbled Wicks, blood running down the side of his mouth, his eyes staring, terrified, into Gant's.

"Easy there, Wicks. You're gonna make it. Your ol' saddle pard, Eli Gant, ain't about to leave you, if that's what you're thinkin'."

Well, not yet, he thought.

"Thanks, Gant," Wicks said gratefully, coughing a spray of blood.

"Now come on, let's get our pal into his saddle," Gant said to the others. Between them, they got him up there but they had to tie him to the saddle horn. Wicks's face had paled, his coughing became harsher and drier. Still they went on, past Black Butte and into the twisting, narrow canyons that lay beyond. When night started to fall Gant called a halt. They dismounted and cut Wicks out of his saddle. The wounded man had only been semi-conscious for the last couple of miles.

Gant had started to worry that he might start babbling and alert any Apaches in the vicinity. After considering it he decided that if Wicks started hollering he'd use his hunting knife to shut him up.

They made a cold camp, drinking water out of their canteens and eating jerky from the saddle-bags. As a precaution Gant tied and gagged Wicks. The bleeding had stopped. They took it in turns to keep a look-out for the posse or the Apaches.

* * *

The posse reached Black Butte a couple of hours after Gant's men had ridden past. Holland decided they had gone far enough in reaching the mark he had set for them; straightaway he got an argument from Kilbourne.

"I say we go on," Kilbourne said to them, when Holland had them dismount.

This surprised Holland. He knew Kilbourne to be a blowhard, but had not reckoned him to be a foolhardy blowhard.

"No, Kilbourne, we've come far enough." Some of the others turned to Kilbourne, waiting for him to challenge the sheriff.

"Why not, Jack? There's still a couple of hours of daylight left. Might catch up with 'em," he said shortly, waiting for support from one of his pals. Nobody spoke up.

Kilbourne went on, "Hell, what about it? Might get a chance to finish it tonight. What about it, Pettifer? You don't want to be away from that wife of yours for too long."

Pettifer's wife was ten years younger than him and took some pleasing in bed; a lot held that Pettifer wasn't up to it.

"Don't worry about her," a voice called from the back, "she won't go cold." They all laughed, except Pettifer who just coloured up. He looked around hoping to identify the voice. The little liveryman had been sweating all afternoon, knowing that at sometime or other they were going to catch up with the gang and there'd be shooting. His clammy hand tightened round his gun. The only reason he'd volunteered for the posse had been in the hope of getting some respect from his barb-tongued wife, as well as hoping she'd cool down if she thought she might get the flat of his hand across her face. If a man went on a posse after Gant, then there was no telling what he might do. Pettifer hoped she'd see it that way.

Licking his lips, he called out,

"Sheriff's right. We go wandering about in the dark we could hit anythin'."

Holland and Kilbourne were surprised at Pettifer's speaking up, neither thought he had the balls for it.

"Besides, we'd better wait and see what Davies has found if he's found anything." Holland found another reason to keep them where they were.

What he didn't want was them blundering into Gant and his men until he knew where they were and what they were up to. If a couple of them got hit quick the rest might take it into their heads to call it quits and go home.

It was dark when Davies came back. Taking Holland to one side, he said, "They're not far ahead. They had to make a stop for Wicks, guy's bleeding pretty bad." He drank from the cup of coffee that Holland had given him.

"Good, that ought to slow them down. Any idea where they're headed?" Holland watched the posse eating the plates of beans, and drinking the cups of coffee they had brewed.

"Border's gettin' pretty close, though I did see Apache signs. That might force them to swing off a bit."

"Thanks, Buck. Git some sleep. An' go out as soon as you're ready in the morning." As Davies went to get some food, Holland did the rounds of the guards he'd posted. When he came back the others had turned in, some of them snoring loudly under their blankets. In his saddle-bag he found the whiskey bottle he had stashed and had a liberal mouthful. Lying down, his hands under his head, he searched the Arizona sky. The stars were everywhere above him. When he had first come to Red Bluff and had started courting Claire, they'd pretend to count the stars in the sky and wish on them. For the first time since becoming a lawman he gave serious thought to bringing in an outlaw over his saddle.

Buck woke him, his hands on his shoulder, shaking him until Holland woke up.

“What is it?” Rubbing his eyes Holland brought the tracker’s face into focus.

“We got a dead man,” Davies said quietly, so as not to wake any of the others.

Holland sat up. “What do you mean?”

“Ben Rixton’s had his throat cut. Sure looks like Apache work.” Davies slipped away leaving the sheriff to follow him.

Ben Rixton had been a handyman around town, doing all the odd jobs that needed doing, helping out Pettifer in the livery, Kilbourne in his forge and Brocklesby in his store.

When Holland got to him, he was staring up at the sky, his throat slashed from side to side. Blood had squirted everywhere, splashing the ground and the rocks behind him.

“Sneaky devils, ain’t they?” Davies closed Rixton’s eyes for him. “Never knew what happened until it had happened.”

"Bastards," swore Holland with feeling. Behind him he heard the first of the posse stirring. This would be the first test of how they'd stand up to losing one of their own. It could be the makings of the posse or it could break it.

Kilbourne sidled over to where they were hunched over Rixton. Yawning and stretching as he came he opened his mouth to say something, then he saw Rixton stretched out on the ground.

"You'd better wake that lazy bastard," he said, "or we're gonna be here all day." Abruptly, he stopped speaking as he saw the slashed throat.

"Christ," he intoned solemnly then turned away from the sight; a few seconds later Holland and Davies heard him throwing up. The sheriff and the tracker exchanged glances.

Kilbourne came back wiping his face with the back of his hand, a green look to his gills. Davies went to waken the rest of the posse. One by one they came over to where Rixton lay, and one by one they all lost their colour.

"What you gonna do, Jack?" Buck Davies asked from the back of his horse.

"One thing for sure, from the way they look," Holland spoke grimly.

Davies furrowed his eyebrows. "What's that?"

"I won't have to get breakfast for them." Holland gave a macabre, quiet laugh.

"Reckon not," Davies said, as he headed out.

Holland proved to be right. None of the posse, except himself, wanted breakfast.

As he bit into the jerky and bread he watched the others as they stood about talking amongst themselves. The shock of what happened in Red Bluff had worn off and the new shock of what had happened to Rixton had just started to sink in. When he had finished eating, Holland went over to the group and called them together.

"You've all seen what's happened to

Rixton." He searched the face of each one. "You didn't come along to fight Apaches, that's an army job; you came along to catch Gant and his men. So there's no hard feelings if any of you wants to turn back."

No one answered immediately, but Frank Brocklesby spoke up in the end. Brocklesby owned the general store and had lived in Red Bluff for ten years with his wife and two daughters. Quietly spoken, he was nevertheless forceful and persistent.

"Doesn't matter whether it's Indians or Gant's sort: we said we'd do a job and we can't go back 'til we've finished it."

"Hold hard," Kilbourne put in. "If there's Apaches I don't see how we can get through them and fight Gant." He shuffled nervously.

"We don't know how many Apaches there are," Brocklesby continued, meeting Kilbourne's eyes. "Besides, you were all for pressing on last night, as I remember," he added sarcastically. Brocklesby didn't think there was cat in hell's chance of catching up with Gant and his boys, but anybody who had been on the posse would have something to sing about, especially when Franz Grossman's term as mayor of Red Bluff came to an end.

"Last night was last night," Kilbourne told him, balling his fists.

Quickly, Holland stepped between the two men, pushing Kilbourne out of the way.

"Simmer down, the pair of you," he snarled; the last thing he wanted was to be in the middle of a posse that was breaking up.

Brocklesby studied those around him. "Well, what about it?" His eyes met those of Pettifer.

"Why're you lookin' at me?" demanded the liveryman, shifting nervously, conscious that they were all watching him.

"'Cos you're part of this posse," Brocklesby told him, "even if you're scared shitless. I've seen you watching the back trail."

Pettifer's face swelled up. "Everybody here's scared," he replied, Brocklesby's goading working as he hoped it would.

"So what's it to be, liveryman? You comin' along or are you hightailin' it back to town knowin' you'll have to face that wife of yours?"

Pettifer, the much smaller man, flung himself at Brocklesby. It took Holland unawares; the two men were on the floor before he could separate them.

Overcoming his surprise, he bent down to grab Pettifer's collar. Wrapping his fist around the rough material, he dragged the man to his feet, then thrust the flat of his hand into Brocklesby's face. Brocklesby had got to his feet wanting to continue the fight, but Holland easily held him off.

"That's it," he shouted. "Any more of it, and I'll put a stop to it."

Silence fell over the posse. Brocklesby appeared shocked by Pettifer's onslaught and Pettifer seemed ready to start again. Guessing Pettifer's motives, Holland said, "You don't have to go through with this; no one'll think any less of you."

The words had no effect on the liveryman, who glared at Brocklesby. "I'm goin' through with this. I don't care what that sidewinder thinks." For him that clinched the matter. One by one the others agreed to go on, including Kilbourne, even though some of them were pretty reluctant.

Watching them saddle up Holland wondered how much more trouble they were going to give him, and how they would react when they came up against the killers and the lead started to fly.

6

BUCK DAVIES didn't envy Jack Holland when he rode out of the camp to pick up the trail of the killers. The posse had all the makings of trouble. That was Jack's responsibility, he reflected. Finding Gant was his chore.

Yesterday had not been as bad as he thought it might be, not with one of them taking a slug and bleeding like a pig fit for butchering. Today would be different. The blood spots petered out early on. A couple of hours after leaving the posse he came across a heap of horse droppings.

Seem pretty fresh, Davies said to himself after he had got down to examine them. He noticed that the length of the strides had been cut down considerably. The horses were getting tired, needing food, a rest and water. Getting to his feet Davies gave the matter some thought. He knew the canyons and the area down to the border pretty well.

There were a few settlements around that the gang could hole up in, and there was a place just this side of the border. He thought hard to remember the name, the kind of place Gant's sort made for. Racking his mind he searched for the name, Last Stop, the outlaw hang-out, the place where they went to trade their loot for supplies and information before heading south into Mexico or coming back north after the heat had died down. Whiskey and women aplenty, he recalled. That's where they'd be headed. Getting to Last Stop would take a few days and, if they got there, Holland and his posse would have to fight the whole town instead of just Gant and his men. Best thing would be to nail them before they got that far.

Davies climbed back into the saddle. Rowelling his horse he urged the palomino forward across the desert.

* * *

"Can't last much longer." Morley gestured towards Wicks who lay on his saddle blanket, beads of shiny sweat covering his gaunt, exhausted face.

"Thought he'd be dead before now." Gant helped himself to a drink from Wicks's canteen. All Wicks had to do was to stay alive long enough for the posse to catch up.

Wicks lay in the shadow of some rocks while his horse stood by picking at the few blades of grass and scrub. A bout of shivering shook his body.

"Hi, Wicks." Gant leaned over him putting the canteen to his quivering lips. "You're lookin' considerably better this mornin'," Gant soft-talked him.

"Don't feel it." Wicks told him mournfully.

"Goin' to be gettin' a doctor to you pretty soon." Sitting down Gant watched Wicks's face to see if he'd swallowed it. He had.

The surprise showed in Wicks's face, "A doc?" He coughed violently, blood running down his stubbly jaw.

"Dak knows where there's a settlement where we can git a doc for ya. Better than bumping along on a horse. It ain't far from here. After that there's gonna be a change of plan," Gent lied easily.

"What sorta change?" Wicks asked eagerly, feeding on the false hope that Gant had spooned him.

"Instead of goin' down to Last Stop, we'll be cuttin' back east to throw the posse," he laughed.

Wicks laughed with him, "Don't that beat all?"

"Sure do, then some." Gant rocked with laughter.

Morley came up, leading the horses.

He gave Wicks a half-empty bottle of whiskey. "This'll keep you company 'til we get back. Gonna ride down the trail a'ways, keep an eye open for Dak.

Make sure he ain't run into them Apaches or nothin'."

Wicks said, "You ain't gonna leave me?"

"Hell no," smooth-talked Gant. "Just gonna make sure Dak gets here in one piece." Climbing into the saddle he and Morley gave Wicks a good-bye wave.

"Dak got a sight of him 'bout a mile back. Comin' up real cautious like. Could tell it was Davies. Still ridin' that ol' palomino he was ridin' last time he tracked us," Morley said as soon as they were out of earshot of Wicks. "Planted himself in some rocks so he can get a good shot at that no-good 'breed."

"Then let's go." Gant's voice had a jovial ring to it.

Morley turned in his saddle, "He buy that horse shit?"

"Every last piece of it. Thinks we're comin' back with a doc. An' I told him we're going back east a'ways. Soon as Holland finds Davies's body, it won't take him long to find Wicks."

They did not take long to get to the rocks where Dak had concealed himself overlooking the trail that Buck Davies must take if he was to find them.

Dismounting, they tethered the horses to a bush. The climb to where Dak overlooked the trail was not a long one, but, by the time they found him lying on his belly, his rifle propped against a rock, they were thirsty and the sweat was oozing from their pores.

Dak looked at them.

"Any sign of him?" Gant squatted down beside him, his own rifle in his hands. Morley got down beside him, squinting hard at the scene below as he levered a shell into the breech.

"No." Dak spat over the ledge and watched the phlegm strike the dust below. The sun cut through their clothes, scorching their backs and making the desert shimmer. A lizard ran across the lip of the rock until Gant flicked it over the edge. Dak wiped the sweat off the edge of his nose.

Suddenly, Dak shifted his position a

bit. "He's comin'."

The three of them pressed themselves further into the dust, hands caressing the stocks of their rifles. Davies rode on, suspecting nothing.

"One shot each ought to do it." Gant moved up a fraction, squinting along the barrel of the rifle. Davies came on, still suspecting nothing.

The heat had made Davies sleepy, so sleepy that he had just about decided to rest for a few minutes when he caught sight of a movement in the rocks ahead of him.

"Now," Gant called out. Simultaneously, three rifles spat lead at Davies. One slug hit him in the forehead, another in the shoulder and Gant's caught him square in the heart. The force of the shots flung him from the saddle. His dead body crashed to the ground.

With a feeling of satisfaction Gant led the others down to the horses; they shoved their rifles into the saddle scabbards, then rode down to where

Davies's body lay. Gant stared at the body, its head shattered, the shirt front blasted open, the blood already drying in the sun.

"Cain't hardly miss him. All they got to do then is find Wicks." Dak ran his fingers through his belt to loosen it against his sweat-drenched waist.

"They'll find Wicks, Holland'll see to that," Gant said hungrily. "An' he'll ride in every direction an' find nothin'."

"Why don't we wait for the posse?" Morley bit himself a hunk of chewing tobacco.

"Don't have to. They're all townies. Useless with a gun. It's Holland I wanted. An' findin' his wife in that bank surely was a stroke of luck. Holland's already dead."

7

JACK HOLLAND strode to the head of the canyon, his binoculars in his hand. Raising them, he scanned the desert ahead, but his thoughts were on his wife, Claire. His grip tightened until his knuckles turned white. He had not really had time to think about her until now. The thoughts burned in him but he tried to push them out of his mind, knowing that if he dwelled on them they would eat him up. He was going to have Gant at the end of a gun or dangling from a rope, whichever came first.

Behind him, the posse stretched out in the shadow of the rocks, taking a breather and a drink from their canteens.

Holland could see nothing ahead of him. Irritated he walked back to the sweating unshaven posse.

"Go easy on that water. Won't be

any more 'til we get to Sandy Wells." Sandy Wells was the hottest and driest part of the desert, and there wasn't always water there.

A couple of heads came up at his tone of voice. Kilbourne especially gave him a sharp look. "We goin' that far after 'em?" He struggled to keep his voice level as he got to his feet. Sleeving his face, and gasping he squinted through the sweat at Holland.

"We're goin' that far, and further — if it takes it," Brocklesby told him, sidling up to Holland's side.

"You suggestin' I ain't up to it?" Kilbourne took a pace forward, his hand balling up.

"He ain't suggestin' nothing of the sort." Holland got quickly between them, anxious to prevent them beating each other to a pulp.

If Gant could see them now, he'd laugh himself sick, he thought. "Saddle up an' let's make some tracks," he shouted to the rest of the posse who were watching things closely.

Lethargically, they got up from the shade and went to their horses. Holland watched them mount, especially Kilbourne and wondered how much longer he'd stick it. They rode out of the canyon, Holland in the lead. They stuck to the trail; if they left it, and got lost in the desert, Holland knew that none of them would get back to Red Bluff without Davies to guide them.

The sooner Buck Davies shows up, the better, he thought.

The tracks left by Gant's crew were becoming harder to follow since leaving Black Butte. A few miles beyond Black Butte they had found a bloodstained bandanna, and Holland guessed that it had been used to patch Wicks up, but since then they had found nothing.

Pettifer rode at the back of the posse. Every so often he glanced nervously over his shoulder, as if expecting to see Gant and his men come charging out of nowhere, their guns blazing.

What the hell did I get involved in this for? he thought sullenly. Damn the bitch. When I get back I'll whip her raw, then see what she does. Damn.

Brocklesby, despite his talk, had started to think along the same lines. Being mayor of a small town in the middle of nowhere sure as hell wasn't worth getting blasted to little pieces for. Grossman can be mayor until hell freezes over.

The sudden halting of the posse took him by surprise. Up ahead he saw Holland draw his pistol and raise his arm. Quickly, Pettifer looked around. No one was behind them. He could not make out what was being said in front of him but Holland had either seen something or felt that something was wrong.

Holland and Kilbourne took off towards the rocks that straddled the trail.

"Sheriff says we're to stay here." Brocklesby had ridden back to them. "Holland and Kilbourne have seen something up ahead. they're gonna see what it is," Brocklesby called out to those who had stayed put.

Heads craned forward as Kilbourne came back rickety split. He reined in his horse just in front of Brocklesby. Kilbourne's face had turned green.

Pettifer felt his belly crawl. Before he could ask, Kilbourne spat out, "Found Davies up there." He pointed to where Holland had hunkered down examining something.

"He hurt bad?" Pettifer heard himself say.

"Dead as hell. All shot to pieces." Kilbourne sounded as though he was going to be sick.

Pettifer wanted to throw up.

Damn it, he thought. I'm going back. I don't care what anybody says.

Brocklesby caught his eye. They were thinking the same thing. Kilbourne looked ready to fall off his horse.

At least I won't be going back alone, thought Pettifer as he watched Kilbourne and Brocklesby.

"Now what's going on?" demanded Brocklesby, wiping his face with his badanna, seeing Holland wave towards them.

"Think he wants us down there," Kilbourne said, obviously not relishing the prospect of going back to view Davies's body. The posse trotted to where Holland stood in the middle of the trail. He stood silently by the bullet-riddled corpse.

"Guess Buck caught up with Gant," Holland said simply.

No one made any reply. They were all thinking the same thing: Any time now, it's gonna be me.

The cold eye of Jack Holland swept over the faces. Buck Davies's body marked the end of the trail without them even getting a sight of Gant.

Kilbourne licked his lips; Brocklesby avoided his eyes; Pettifer turned away. There was a long silence.

"You boys go back if you want. This ain't a job for ordinary citizens. It needs regular deputies or gunmen."

The words stuck in Holland's throat. The people of the town had let him down, and they all knew it.

"Better take Davies's body with you," Holland told them. Nobody said anything as they slung the tracker's body over his saddle.

Kilbourne turned as they rode away, "No hard feelings, Jack."

Shaking his head Holland watched them as they rode back to Red Bluff, a red-hot storm building up inside him. He stood there as they disappeared from sight.

The way Holland figured it, the shots must have come from overhead. A rock arch spread over the trail, tailing down to the open ground. Going round, Holland found the place where they'd tethered the horses and bootprints of the men over the rocky ground.

Mounting the bay, he let the animal walk down the trail, his gun in his hand, eyes and senses alert. Nothing moved save the flies swarming and buzzing round the bay's tail. Some sixth sense prevented him from going on.

Dismounting, he tied his horse to a bush. Although he could not see it clearly, something moved near the rock.

Cocking his pistol, Holland edged towards it. Suddenly, a single shot cut the air and he felt the bullet pluck at his sleeve. Holland flung a shot towards the puff of gunsmoke and rolled sideways to confuse the mysterious gunman. A second shot sliced into the ground to his left, well away from him.

Belly down, hugging the dry ground, Holland inched forward. Another shot sang out, even further to his left. Holland started to squeeze the trigger of his gun when he stopped himself. Whoever it was was out there alone, without any clear view of him. Holding his fire Holland decided not to give his position away. Instead, he continued to move forward until he could see the half-conscious body of Wicks, his head rolling from side to side.

Seizing the opportunity, Holland

leapt to his feet and ran towards Wicks. As he reached him, he kicked the gun from his hand.

As Holland picked up the gun, Wicks opened his eyes. "Hi, Holland," he croaked.

Holland's gaze rolled over one of his wife's killers. The rage swelled up inside him and before he could stop himself, he grabbed Wicks by the throat, dragging him to his feet and struck him across the head with his pistol. The he let Wicks fall.

"Where are they?" Holland stood over Wicks, his gun trembling in his hand, at the very edge of self-control.

"What're'y' gonna do, Sheriff Holland, kill me?" Wicks's voice was feeble and hoarse and Holland could see that he didn't have long.

"Where are they?" repeated Holland.

"Let me finish that whiskey an' I'll think about it," Wicks laughed hoarsely.

Reluctantly, Holland picked up the near empty whiskey bottle and held it out. Then he pulled it away.

"All right. They were headin' for Last Stop, but Gant changed his mind. They're headin' due east. Aimin' to throw you. Now, can I have that whiskey. Please." The last word was a mixture of sarcasm and contempt.

Holland handed him the bottle. Wicks spat out the cork an put it to his lips. When he glanced at Holland again, he was on his horse.

"Ain't you gonna take me in?" he croaked.

"No," Holland told him. "Gonna let the sun or the Apaches do my dirty work for me."

8

LAST STOP lay sprawled across the desert, a haphazard selection of houses and general stores built around a clutter of saloons. It had everything that a regular town had, general store, livery stable, saloons, cat houses everything except a sheriff's office. The town had no need for the law and the law had no use for Last Stop.

Once an outlaw got inside the city limits he was as good as across the border. It would have needed a small army to clean out the hell-hole.

Last Stop was Gant's kind of place. He, Morley and Dak could trade booty, spend their stolen money or buy information as to what the law was doing on the outside.

Just one rule held sway in Last Stop: don't steal from your own kind. If a man brought in a bunch of money, it was his, no question. If anybody else put a claim on it, he got a bullet in the back. That's why Gant's kind used Last Stop. It gave them a breather before crossing the border.

The three of them rode in about midmorning and headed for the Lucky Lady. As they dismounted and tied their horses to the hitch rail, a familiar sound of argumentative voices reached them through the batwings.

"'N I say you're a cheatin' bastard, Silas Faulds," barked a tall, rangy Texan with a pair of guns tied down low on his hip.

Gant and the others moved back against the wall out of the line of fire. The tall Texan and the elegantly dressed Silas Faulds faced each other across a table with cards and greenbacks scattered all over it. Faulds, the owner of the Lucky Lady, wore his guns tied down beneath a long morning coat. His face carried an expression of injured innocence.

"No, Billy Boy, I ain't cheating. The

way you play I don't have to." As he spoke his hands pushed back the flap of his coat. To everybody except Billy, it was obvious that the tone of voice and the remark were calculated to distract the Texan from the movements of Faulds' hands and to cause him to lose his temper.

"You sayin' I cain't play cards?" Billy's face reddened under Faulds' silky-voiced insult.

"No, I ain't sayin' that: I'm sayin' you don't know the difference between four aces an' three." As these last words came out of Faulds' mouth, his right hand moved like a striking snake. His gun came up in his hand, the thumb drawing back the hammer, the loud explosion splitting the silence of the room. The bullet smashed into Billy's chest like a hammer blow, flinging him backwards so that his body overturned the chairs behind him.

Billy died before his gun cleared leather. He lay wide-eyed, staring at the ceiling.

Dropping his gun back into his holster, Silas Faulds' eyes challenged everybody in the saloon. When no one else took up the challenge he said, "Drinks on the house. Boys," he called to the barkeeps, then jerked a thumb at Billy, "clean this mess up."

A moment later the two barkeeps were dragging Billy's corpse out of the saloon. The spectators roared their approval then swarmed for the bar.

Seeing Gant, Morley and Dak, Faulds went across, his hands outstretched in greeting, an oily smile on his lips.

"Up to your old tricks?" Morley greeted him.

"Don't know what you mean," Faulds laughed, backslapping them to the bar and waving for three beers to be served to the parched outlaws.

"Betcha don't," growled Dak, elbowing two cowboys out of his way. They both turned, hard expressions on their faces but, when they saw his size and girth, they hurriedly finished their drinks and pushed their way out of the bar.

"What can I do for you boys?" Faulds asked, wrapping his hand around a beer glass.

"We wanna put up here for a couple days. We're headin' south. Nogales, maybe. We got some stuff to trade. Interested?" Gant took a long pull at the beer and wiped the froth from his mouth, all the time watching Faulds' face.

"What kind a stuff? Been gettin' a lot through here lately," he told Gant.

"Was there ever a time when you wasn't gettin' any stuff through?" Gant nodded at the others. "Me an' the boys know you're a bigger thief than us." The three of them laughed. Faulds just carried on watching them.

Tapping the saddle-bags which he had thrown on the bar, Gant said, "Got rings, watches, necklaces. Makes our hearts bleed to let you have the stuff for next to nothin'."

Faulds laughed sharply and threw back his head. "C'mon, bring it through to the office an' I'll take a look at it."

They followed Faulds through to his office, passing cases of whiskey which were piled along the walls.

When they got to the office Faulds unlocked the door. Inside, he struck a match and lit the lamp that stood on the desk in the middle of the room.

While Gant unstrapped the saddle-bags, Morley eyed up the safe. It was the one that Faulds had been using for years. He smiled inwardly. Could always depend on Faulds, he thought.

"Say," asked Faulds suddenly, "where's Wicks? He gone out on his own account?"

"Could say that," Gant laughed cruelly. "Caught a bellyful of lead on the last job. Poor boy just bled to death in my arms." He tipped the stuff on the table.

Faulds' eyes lit up as he gave a whistle. Pawing the jewellery, he took a glass from his pocket and screwed it into his eye. For a few minutes he examined the stuff while the others helped themselves to his whiskey.

"Right handsome haul, Eli."

"Glad you like it," Dak said, reaching for the bottle to replenish his glass.

Picking up a wad of bills held together by a brown wrapper, Faulds read the lettering. "You fellas hit Red Bluff?"

"We hit Red Bluff," Morley told him, his eyes never leaving the stash on the table. "Why?" he asked suspiciously.

"Fella came through this morning. You sure made a hell of a mess of the place." Faulds blew smoke in the direction of the safe.

"Meant to," Gant told him. "Just paying 'em back for Mordecai. Here's to Mordecai." He raised his glass. The others did likewise.

"I'll give you a price for this stuff in the morning," Faulds said, when he had finished inspecting it. Pushing back the chair he stood up, his thumb hooked into his pocket, a freshly lit cheroot dangling from his fingers.

Gant, Morley and Dak finished their drinks and went to the door.

"Now, you boys git out there and git a few drinks, enjoy a few of the girls," Faulds told them with a wide-faced grin as he waved them out of his office.

In the corridor Morley spat into the sawdust, his face screwed up in a twisted sneer. "He's gonna give us a quarter of what that stuff's worth," he snorted.

Back in the saloon they lined up against the bar which was covered in rings where wet glasses had stood. Behind them was the table where the Texas boy had been playing against Faulds. By now it was all cleaned up and fresh sawdust spread over the floor to cover the bloodstains. Four other men were trying their luck with the cards.

Gant ordered three beers. After a few minutes he turned to watch the play. Then he saw that a fresh game was about to start up. "I'm gonna try my luck at the cards," he announced. "You boys comin'?"

"Nah," Dak said.

Morley grunted a refusal and shook his head. Crossing the floor Gant sat down on an empty chair. The other three players looked at each other, then nodded. A second later the cards started to float across the table.

"See that filly in the green dress?" Dak asked.

"Sure I see her," Morley told him, following the giant's gaze to the far end of the saloon where the girl and a companion sat talking as they waited for customers.

"Reckon to buy some of her time; you game to take on her friend?" Dak leered, his lust-filled eyes roaming over the whore.

"Just too worn out. Gonna have a few beers then hit the sack," Morley said as he looked into his glass.

"Be seein' you," Dak said, as he put down the glass with a thump.

"Yeah, be seein' you." Morley

signalled the barkeep for a refill. He watched Dak moving in on the whore. Through the mirror he could see Gant getting ready to deal the cards.

Dropping coins on the counter he took the top off the beer. The saddle-bags with the stash in them were safely locked in Faulds' safe. Sometime in the next couple of days he would have to get into that safe and lift the saddle-bags and high-tail it over the border to meet up with Belle. The question was how?

Ruminating on it, he did not notice the tall well-dressed stranger until the stranger collided with him, half-emptying his beer on the bar. Morley faced the stranger ready to settle the matter with fists or guns. Instead of getting an argument or any kind of trouble, Morley got a smiling apology.

"I beg your pardon," the stranger said with a courtesy that Morley was not used to. "Allow me to buy you another beer." The smile and the offer of another beer left Morley at a loss for words.

"That's plumb decent of you," Morley said, taking the opportunity of sizing up the man. His clothes were those of a gambler, white ruff-fronted shirt with a diamond pin in the front, striped trousers, brown tooled-leather boots. He carried a black cane and wore a broad-brimmed panama hat.

He signalled for the barkeep to bring over a couple of beers and told him to keep the change.

"Well," he said, pointing to a table on the other side of the saloon, "a game of poker calls and who am I to ignore it?" He touched the brim of his hat and sauntered off, glass in hand.

"Say, I was wondering who the snappy dresser was," said Morley, buttonholing the barkeep when he came over to replenish his glass.

"That's Mark Lucas, big gambler from outa town," he replied.

Snorting, Morley took the head off

the beer. "Big gambler in a place like this?"

The barkeep shrugged. "Biggest game in the county bein' played tomorrow night at the Three Aces. Butler and Faulds are takin' a hand as well as Lucas. Most of the town's gonna be there to see a lotta greenbacks change partners."

"You don't say," Morley told him thoughtfully.

"I do say. This place is gonna be pretty quiet, everybody's gonna be over at the Three Aces." With that he walked away to serve somebody else.

Morley took his time finishing his drink. Gant was still sliding the cards across the table, Dak had taken the girl upstairs. He went outside. So that's how it's going to be, he thought. Nearly everybody in town would be in the Three Aces. Faulds' place, Lucky Lady, would be almost deserted. Morley walked to the end of the block. A narrow alley ran down the side of the saloon. It was a cinch that there would be a window at the back. Just snap the catch and climb in. He turned back through the batwings.

9

THE place had no name, at least Holland didn't see any signpost that told him the name of the hamlet he was riding into. If he hadn't seen the dim cluster of lights he would have ridden past it in the dark.

Two days had passed since he and the posse had parted company. His anger at their departure had diminished to dull resentment. Being honest, he could not blame them: Gant's men were professional killers, well versed in the ways of violent death. The men who had volunteered for the posse, with the exception of Buck Davies, were ordinary citizens trying to make an honest living for their families, yet he could not help feeling that they should have stuck with him. At the same time he was glad he was on his own and not responsible for their safety.

Shortly after watching them ride out, he had taken the tin star off his vest and dropped it in the dust. On the two days alone on the trail, he had come to feel the loss of Claire. Never had he felt so alone.

A voice from the dark jogged him from his reverie.

"Say, watch where you're goin'."

"Sorry fella," Holland called out. Below him, swaying in the dark, stood a figure dressed in range clothes. The man staggered out of the way, obviously drunk.

Holland shouted after him. "Say what's the name of this place?"

The cowboy came back towards him, having difficulty keeping his feet.

"Name of the place?" He thought hard, scratching his head as he did so. Then his face lit up. "Ain't got a name. None that I ever heard of an' I've been here for a couple of years."

Before Holland could ask him if there was any place he could bed down, the cowboy had staggered off.

Ahead of him, Holland could make out the building from where most of the light was coming. He hauled the bay's head around and nudged her flanks.

There were no other horses at the hitch rail. Dismounting, Holland approached the door. As he went in he picked up several different smells, mostly bad whiskey, worse food, all mingled with the smell of unwashed bodies. Inside three lamps cast a meagre light over what seemed to be a saloon-cum-store. Conversation ceased as half a dozen heads swung in his direction.

A big man stood behind the counter, his ham-sized fists resting on the top.

"What'll it be?" His booming voice echoed round the room.

"Beer an' something to eat," Holland replied, feeling in his pockets for some money.

"We got it," the big man answered. "Potatoes, steak, beans. But we ain't got ice-cream an' apple pie. You want it?" The men at the table behind

Holland laughed.

Holland nodded. "Yeah. I want it."

"Hey, Blair," called out one of the men from the table, "if he ain't having ice cream and apple pie, maybe he'll have Ally?" Blair and the three men laughed. As they did so Holland caught sight of a woman sitting on a chair at the far end of the bar, her chin resting on the palm of her hand.

"What about it, fella? You want a piece of Ally? It's free." They all laughed again. The girl's face remained expressionless. Holland turned and walked to the back of the room and sat down to await the food. A couple of minutes later Blair came across with his beer.

For a while he watched the three men playing stud poker. Every now and then one of them would throw a look his way. The girl remained, motionless, where she was. Blair just leaned on the counter, sometimes rubbing a cloth up and down.

Finishing the beer and seeing no sign

of the food coming Holland got up and went to the bar.

"Another?" Blair asked, holding up a glass.

"Might as well," Holland replied, shortly.

While Blair was pulling the drink one of the card players came to stand by his elbow.

"Something troubling you, fella?" Holland asked, picking up his glass and turning to face the man.

"Got a familiar look to you, that's all," the man, who wore a yellow shirt, said. "Got a name?"

"Jack Holland. What's yours?" Holland figured that the best way to deal with him was to be as aggressive as he was. He put the glass down, and let his hand crawl down to his gun butt.

"No need for that," the man said, watching Holland's hand. "Name's Tom Cooper. No, guess I musta made a mistake." Without another word he walked back to the card game.

Picking up his drink Holland made

his way back to his table. As he passed he caught the look on Cooper's face. The man was not entirely satisfied that he did not know Holland. And well he might. Holland sat down. The moment he got a good look at the three faces Holland remembered them. Tom Cooper: so the others must be Billy Horn and Milt Sherwood. Holland had been in a posse that the four had outrun to get across the Mexican border some years back when Holland had just started sheriffing.

While the thought was passing through his mind the door opposite opened and a crone shuffled in holding a tray with his food on it. The food was as unappetising as Holland had feared it might be. He ate it slowly while he drank his beer. The card players and Blair threw him the occasional suspicious look. Having finished his meal Holland went to the bar.

"Ever heard of a place called Last Stop?" he asked. Immediately the place became silent.

"Last Stop?" Blair threw a glance at the card players whose play had suddenly stopped. The girl at the end of the bar looked Holland's way.

"I asked if you had heard of Last Stop," Holland repeated.

"An' if I have?" Blair's eyes never left those of the other three.

"I'd sure appreciate some directions," Holland said slowly, sensing the quickening interest behind him.

"Now why would a fella wish to go to Last Stop?" Cooper asked, coming across the room.

"Same reason as you, I dare say." Holland stared directly into Cooper's eyes.

Cooper let out a loud guffaw. "Knew I'd seen you before, pilgrim. So, you're on the dodge as well?"

Holland blessed his stars. All right if that's what they wanted to think, he'd let them. "Sure, I'm on the dodge."

"You've come to the right place. That's where me an' the boys are headed. That right boys?" he asked with a wide grin.

"That's right, Tom," Milt Sherwood chimed in. "Me an' the boys are just in front of a posse. Had to stop here before the horses died under us. We'll be pullin' out in the mornin'. You can ride with us. OK, boys?" Sherwood asked the others. "I'm Milt Sherwood."

"OK by me," Billy Horn said.

"Thanks." Holland looked around the room; the girl at the end of the bar had said nothing, but he had the feeling that she was watching him and taking in every word that was said.

"There's a livery out the back if you want to bed your horse down." Blair cocked a thumb in the direction of the barn.

Outside, Holland found the livery. The place was empty so he figured that the fella who ran it had gone off for the night, not thinking it likely that anybody would come in so late. Rubbing the bay down Holland fed it and then led it into a stall where he left it. In the bar the three outlaws were still playing stud poker, Blair and the crone were still behind the bar and the girl was still sitting on the chair, saying nothing.

"Got a bed for the night?" Holland asked Blair, seeing that it looked as though the others might be up all night playing poker.

"Sorry, fella, that's one thing I'm fresh out of — beds." Blair made an expansive gesture.

The girl at the end of the bar spoke up. "Guess you'd better come in with me."

The suggestion took Holland aback. The girl had not spoken since he had come into the place and she certainly didn't have the set of a whore.

"The man's blushing," Milt Sherwood called out.

Blair laughed. "By God, so he is. Well, fella, it's Ally's bed or the floor. But you'll be safe with Ally." The crone by his side cackled.

"Come on, fella. Let's get some sleep." Ally spoke for the first time. Her voice surprised him. It was soft; the sort of voice he would have expected in a drawing-room, not a hole in the wall.

She went to the foot of the stairs. "Come on, I'm tired as well."

10

ALLY led him up stairs which were narrow and dark and wound round to the rear of the building. Both held lamps so Holland was better able to appreciate the curves of her body and her long, chestnut-coloured hair as he followed her. The stairs were badly constructed and creaked as they went up. She stopped outside a door and opened it. The light of the lamps illuminated the untidy interior. A brass double bed stood against the far end of the wall and by it, under the window, a small table on which she had put her lamp. "You can leave your rig there." She pointed to a chair against the far wall. "Blair and the others won't trouble you as long as they think you're one of them," she said coolly.

Holland's eyebrows went up. "*Think*

I'm one of them? What do you mean?" He started to unstrap his rig.

"I don't know who you are or what you are, but you ain't an outlaw. At least you ain't got that hunted look about you that most of them have."

Holland put the lamp on the table beside Ally's.

"You sound pretty sure of yourself," he told her.

"I am," was her reply. She unfastened the front of her dress, then, looking at Holland, "You can either turn round or you can watch. I don't mind." Pushing the dress over her shoulders she let it drop to the floor, then she kicked it away. Despite his recent loss, Holland could not take his eyes off the girl. Her figure was full, bordering on the voluptuous.

"I'm glad you didn't turn away. I might have taken it the wrong way," she told him as she slipped off her shift and let it fall to the floor.

As he peeled off his own clothes Holland saw she was watching him. Ally had taken a pillow and put it behind her head and was leaning against it, her arms folded across her pink-tipped breasts.

Sitting next to her, Holland could smell the animal scent of her body.

"What's troubling you?" he asked, seeing her eyes on him.

"You are, Jack Holland. Why did you say you were on the dodge when it's plain that you ain't?"

For a moment Holland said nothing, but then the feeling that he could trust her came over him. As a sheriff, he had sometimes had to make decisions on the spur of the moment, when a man might live or die by those decisions. He proceeded to tell her about Red Bluff, Claire, Saul and Gant, the whole thing. She did not interrupt him, but let him finish. Then she simply said "That's a mighty interesting tale."

"Ain't it. What about you? How come you ended up in a place like this?"

Ally snorted. "It was my own fault.

I wanted to come West and see some of this country. So I took up with a wagon train, run by Greg Farmer. He was OK at first, then he started trying it on. Must have thought I was a pushover, travelling by myself. Well, I told him I wasn't an' he got nasty. When we came to this place he told folks I'd been stealing money off him. So they left me here without a bean. Blair put me up for a bit. Said he didn't want no money. Like a fool I believed him." She stopped for a moment. "Then he stuck me with a bill. An' I've been working it off ever since. You know how. Well, tonight, Jack Holland, you're gonna wipe the slate clean for me. And get me a horse and saddle. That was part of the deal. I get a horse and saddle when it was all over. So, tomorrow I ride out of here."

Holland gave her a perplexed look. "Where are you going to go?"

"I haven't thought that far ahead, but I'm going." She twisted a strand of her chestnut hair around her finger.

"You'd best travel with us 'til we get to Last Stop," he advised her.

"Then?" she asked him.

"I haven't thought that far ahead, but when we get there we'll think of something. You can't travel alone through this country. It's downright dangerous."

"You're telling me," she replied. She leaned over quickly and kissed him. Much to his surprise Holland felt the old urge rise in him. Pulling her down on top of him his arms circled her soft body. Strangely, Holland did not feel that he was betraying Claire in any way. As much as he thought about it, he decided that life had to go on. Gant had to be caught and killed, the girl in his arms had to be helped and, if she wanted to show her gratitude, he was a man after all. At last they slept, Ally pushed up close to him for protection.

* * *

Being the first to wake, Holland washed and shaved from the water in the jug. Ally slept soundly, her breasts rising and falling as she breathed. From below he could hear movement, and guessed that Blair was up and about. He decided to go in search of some breakfast.

He found the man still behind the counter.

"How about some breakfast?" he said sharply, seeing the knowing grin on Blair's face.

"Will that be breakfast for two?" he asked slyly.

"That'll be breakfast for two," Holland replied, "and when you've done that you can saddle a horse for the girl. She's paid her dues."

"Meanin'?" Blair's voice took on a surprised tone.

"Meanin' she's leavin' with us." Holland rose from the chair where he had been sitting.

The old crone appeared from what passed as a kitchen. Giving both men a quick look she went back the way she had come.

Throwing down the towel on the counter, Blair came round to Holland's side, his fist balled, ready for trouble.

"You ain't takin' that bitch nowhere," he said grimly. "She's pullin' in customers from miles around. Best thing that ever happened to this god-forsaken hole." His grin bared a mouth of rotting teeth. "An' she ain't goin' nowhere."

"She's goin' with me," Holland told him, with an air of finality in his voice.

Licking his lips, Blair took a step forward and threw a punch at Holland. Blocking it, Holland struck out at Blair's gut. He felt the punch land and sink into the soft flesh, but it seemed to have no effect on the man. Instead, Blair spat into the palms of his hands and came on again.

Feigning a punch at Holland's head he kicked out at his groin. Dropping his hands Holland took the kick on them. The force drove him back into the corner where Blair tried to trap him. Blows rained down on Holland, but he was able to take most of them on his arms. Blair staggered back to take a breath of air. Using the break, Holland danced out of the corner and gave himself more space.

Gathering himself, Blair came at Holland again, swinging wildly, a murderous gleam in his eyes. Holland grabbed a chair and swung it at Blair's head. With one swipe Blair swept it from Holland's hands, so that it went skittering into the corner of the room. He launched himself at Holland, wrapping his huge arms around Holland's waist. The pair of them crashed to the floor, with Blair doing his damnedest to get his fingers around his opponent's throat.

Gasping, Holland took hold of Blair's wrists and slowly forced him upwards. Blair's head crashed into Holland's face so that the room exploded in a shower of bright lights. On his feet, Blair aimed a flurry of kicks at Holland's ribs, but Holland swivelled himself on his back so that the kicks missed. His hand caught the leg of the chair. He swept it round, striking it hard against Blair's legs, sweeping them from under him so that Blair fell heavily to the floor. Seizing his opportunity, Holland got to his feet, his head spinning from Blair's butt.

He shoulder-charged Blair, whose face was covered in blood and matted hair. The force of the charge sent Blair hurtling across the room, crashing into the counter. Determined not to give him any respite, Holland took hold of the chair and swung it against Blair's head. It splintered and Blair collapsed with a moan.

"Been enjoyin' yourselves, boys?" Tom Cooper stood in the doorway of the room surveying the wreck of Blair's face and the damage wrought by the two men.

Holland was breathing hard and his body was aching where Blair had landed telling punches. “Could say that,” he gasped, holding his side.

“You ridin’ out with us?” Cooper came into the room followed by the other two.

Holland watched Blair as he got to his feet. “Just as soon as we’ve had some breakfast.” Hauling up a chair he sat down. “And as soon as Blair’s saddled a horse for Ally.”

“You bringin’ the girl along with you?” Sherwood asked, an anticipatory look on his face.

Guessing that he was going to have trouble, Holland said, “Sure. That all right with you?”

“Jimdandy by me,” Sherwood said with a smile, as he rubbed his hands. It was obvious what he was thinking.

On his feet by now, Blair started putting the place to rights, giving Holland an occasional hard look. He put the chairs upright, then the tables.

“Fix us some breakfast,” Holland told him, “and fix some for the girl.”

With a surly grimace on his face Blair shuffled off to the kitchen.

The others sat down opposite Holland. "You know," Cooper started to say, "more I think about you, the more I think we've met someplace." He pulled out the makings and started to fashion a stogie, then handed the stuff to the others.

"Don't reckon so," Holland replied, curling up inside a little.

With a thoughtful look on his unshaven face, Cooper lit the stogie, and the banner of smoke that he exhaled floated past Holland's head. His eyes never left Holland's.

There was a clumping on the stairs. They all turned their heads as Ally came down, dressed for riding in a pair of levis and a check shirt clinging to her full figure like a limpet. Holland could almost hear what the others were thinking.

"What was all the noise?" she asked sitting down.

"Just our landlord and Jack here,

settling their differences," Horn said. "Something about a horse and saddle."

Ally gave Holland a surprised look. "You've managed to get Blair to give me a horse and a saddle?"

"Sure, but he had to fight him for it." Horn ran his eyes over her once again. "Expect you'll be right grateful to him. Ain't that right, missy?" Horn reached cross the table and tried to put his hand on Ally's. Quickly, she pulled her hand away.

"Jack will tell me if there's anything to pay," she said.

"Sure he will," Horn said, unabashed. "Two days and two nights to Last Stop. Reckon we'll all find out how much there is to pay." He laughed.

The kitchen door opened and the crone came in holding the plates of food, which to Holland seemed to be the warmed-up remains of the previous night's meal.

"Coffee?" she croaked. When Holland nodded, she returned to the kitchen.

The coffee that she brought was no

better than the food she had served them with a few minutes earlier.

Cooper, Horn and Sherwood went outside to give their horses one final tending to and to ensure they had an extra canteen of water. A few minutes later he saw Blair going out the back way.

This could be a rougher trip than I thought, Holland said to himself, as he speared a piece of steak and guided it to his mouth.

Blair returned to his place behind the counter, his face starting to swell, malevolence burning in his eyes. Holland wondered what, if anything, he had been up to while he had been outside with the others.

They finished their breakfast and Holland went over to Blair, his hand in his pocket. He threw some money on the counter.

"That should cover it," he told Blair, watching the man's face for any sign of violence.

"Yeah, that should cover it." Blair's

eyes locked on his. Holland had the cold feeling that something had gone on between him and the others when he had been outside.

"Let's go," he called to Ally, who got up from the table with pure hatred for Blair in her eyes.

Outside they found the other three mounted, waiting for them.

"Let's git goin'." Cooper hauled on his horse's leathers.

11

THE sun was as hot as on any other day that Holland could remember. It burned down out of a blue, cloudless sky, burning everything that lay beneath it. Holland's party left the nameless town at a slow walk. They all knew the folly of pushing the horses in the almost unbearable heat and before moving out, for his own peace of mind, Holland had checked the canteens, ensuring that they were full. It was only when he got to the last one that Cooper took it off his saddle horn and shook it. "No need to check this one," he laughed, "it's full."

Something in the tone of his voice worried Holland, but there was no time to argue about it with him. Instead, he mounted his bay standing next to Ally's horse. They moved off, slowly but steadily under the merciless sun.

None of them spoke, but Holland once or twice detected a surreptitious glance directed at Ally from Cooper. As the sun climbed higher, the slower became their progress, until at last Holland halted them and pointed to a stand of rocks in the distance. "We'll rest there until the sun goes down a bit," he told them.

"Won't get an argument from me," sang out Cooper.

They pushed on towards the rocks. The trail led up a narrow gully where the shade was plentiful. Holland got down from the back of the sweating bay. A gentlemanly instinct made him help Ally down.

"Sure wish I could get my hands on a pair of hips like that," Cooper chuckled throatily. As he did so, Holland noticed him passing his canteen to Sherwood. Sherwood took a long swallow and handed it to Horn who, likewise, helped himself to a long mouthful.

"Go easy on the water," Holland warned them.

Cooper grinned. "Who says it's water?"

Holland strode quickly to the group and pulled the canteen from Horn's hands. He sniffed it.

"You stupid bastards," he shouted. "This is whiskey. It'll dry you faster than anything else. You'll soon use up the water," he snapped.

"An' what if we do?" shouted Cooper. "It's our water."

"Sure an' I hope you remember that if one of the horses has an accident and somebody has to walk."

Cooper tried to push himself to his feet, but fell back against a rock. Sherwood and Horn laughed as they tried to help him up. Instead, they all fell in a heap.

Wiping his forehead. Holland fumed inwardly. The sooner they reached their destination the better. In the meantime he'd better keep an eye on the water, and Ally.

The sun still beat down fiercely. Cooper, Sherwood and Horn dozed in its heat, which relieved Holland from the bother of having to keep an eye on them. At length the sun sank sufficiently for the temperature to come down.

Kicking the others awake, he told them to get mounted, which they did, if somewhat groggily. The three men lolled in their saddles as they rode and Holland knew they were having trouble keeping awake in the heat and would soon be gasping for a drink of water. He wondered how much of the whiskey was left in the spare canteen. There must be a fair amount, he thought. The sooner they drank it the better. Until then he'd just have to keep an eye on them.

Cooper hauled his canteen off his saddle horn and unscrewed the top. Putting it to his lips, he tilted back his head and let the water run down his throat. Some of it ran down the corner of his mouth. Holland cursed the waste of the water they might need if any accident befell them.

Turning, Cooper called out. "What are you starin' at, Holland? Ain't that woman eyeful enough for you?"

"Let's just keep movin', Cooper," Holland called back. "The longer we're out here, the sooner you're going to get through your water."

"You've got plenty." Cooper's voice had a menacing edge to it.

"Ain't all he got," put in Sherwood, looking at Ally lustfully. The two men laughed and then fell silent.

"Bet he's keeping it warm for tonight," Horn chipped in.

"Best be careful, missy. There's more than one kind of rattler out here."

Ally said nothing while all this was going on but Holland could see that it was bothering her. The best thing, he figured, would be to let it ride and hope they'd get tired of mouthing off in Ally's direction. As the afternoon wore on and the first sprinkling of darkness started to fall, it seemed as though things could be working out that way.

"How about calling a halt? These horses are getting plumb wore out," Sherwood called out at last.

"Sure seems that way to me," Horn agreed.

They reigned in their horses just as the sun was balancing on the edge of the horizon. They dismounted near some spiny saguaro, and hobbled the horses. There were enough dead plants and pieces of wood for Holland to gather for a small fire. He did not think it worthwhile to ask the other three to help and Ally's face showed the strain of the near day-long ride.

Holland wandered further from the group than he intended in his search for something with which to build the fire when suddenly, Ally's shriek made him drop the wood and run back to where he had left her. As he approached the group, he drew his gun and cocked it. In the fading light, he saw the men standing round the crouching figure of Ally.

"What's going on?" he demanded,

pushing his way between Ally and the men. From their breath he could tell that they had been drinking.

"Rattler made the little lady jump." Cooper's voice was slurred with the drink.

Grabbing him by the shirt front. Holland lashed him across the head with his gun. Cooper reeled back and fell to the ground, blood spurting from the side of his head.

The other two, deterred by the sight of Holland's gun and the speed of his action, made no attempt to interfere.

"Now," demanded Holland, "where's that bottle?"

"None of your damned business." Cooper struggled to his feet, sleeving away the blood.

"Where is it?" Holland demanded again, taking a step forward towards the three men.

They all exchanged quick glances.

"I'll ask you once more?" Holland's voice had grown threatening as he raised his gun.

Finally, Milt Sherwood gave way. "It's in my saddle-bag."

"Get it," Holland told him. He watched as Sherwood went across to where their horses had been hobbled.

"You two, give me your guns," he told the others. The men hesitated, but Holland was in no mood to wait. He snatched both guns from the holsters. Sherwood came back holding the bottle.

"On the ground with it." Sherwood put the bottle down. Holland put a shot into it. It exploded in a dozen pieces. Slowly, the whiskey seeped into the ground much to the disgust of Sherwood, Cooper and Horn.

"Pure waste," Cooper muttered, watching the whiskey disappear.

Relieving Sherwood of his gun, Holland gestured for them all to get back a few feet.

"You bunk down over there near that big cactus." He pointed to the saguaro a few yards away. The three men walked away in silence, throwing

Holland the occasional baleful glance.

"You all right?" was the first thing he said to the shaken girl.

"You got back just in time," she told him, pushing back the hank of the chestnut-coloured hair.

"I don't think they'll try anything again. Besides, I've got their guns now." Taking them from his belt, Holland put them in his saddle-bag. A few yards away another fire began to lick at the evening sky, the silhouettes of the three men visible against it.

There was bread and meat in the saddlebag that Blair had put there before his fight with Holland. Opening up the package, Holland handed some to Ally.

"Good?" he asked, filling the pot with water to make some coffee.

"Passable," she laughed and then became silent. For a moment she chewed the bread, then looked across the fire at Holland, "What are you going to do when you've caught up with Gant?"

"You mean after I've killed him?" he corrected her.

Ally gulped at the coldness of his tone.

"Yes, I mean after you've killed him." She swallowed the mouthful of food that she was chewing.

Now, it was Holland's turn to be silent. He turned his attention to the sky; it was clear and the night still warm.

"Can't rightly say." His eyes scanned the stars. "No, I can't rightly say."

They both became silent. Holland thought of his slain wife, Ally of the cruel use of her body by Blair and the devilish bargain that he had forced her into.

"Can you use a gun?" Holland asked, as she was about to turn in.

"Sure. Pa was in the cavalry. He made sure I could use a gun. Why?" She refilled their cups from the coffee pot.

Nodding his head in the direction of the others, Holland said, "I'm going to give you Cooper's — just in case. Now, you get some sleep; I'll waken you in a couple of hours."

"OK," she said with a smile.

He watched her bed down, pulling the saddle blanket over her body and using the saddle for a pillow.

Yawning, Holland turned his attention to the other camp fire. From what he could see the others had bedded down for the night as well, their fire just a bunch of embers in the dark of the desert night.

Nothing moved in the dark, but Holland kept his eyes open and his senses alert for any sign of trouble from the others. After a couple of hours he woke Ally so that he could get a few hours' sleep.

The following morning they moved on. Last Stop was just a day and night away. They still remained in two separate groups, Cooper's party making no move to speak. Holland wondered if they were going to try something again with Ally and kept an eye on them.

Just before midday Cooper raised his hand indicating that he wanted them to stop.

"Getting too hot to be going much further. Let's give the horses a breather," he said after he had ridden back a little.

"Can't quarrel with that," Holland told him, sliding out of the saddle. "Best keep an eye on them, Ally," he said, as soon as Cooper was out of earshot.

"Right, Jack," she said touching the waistband of her levis where she had put the gun that Holland had given her.

They settled in the shade of a giant saguaro. Raising his eyes Holland guessed that it might have been about 200 years old. It was about fifty feet high he estimated. Its height and weight had an intimidating effect on him.

The heat caused him to yawn and feel sleepy; the lost hours and the strain of trailing Gant was telling on him. Before he realized it, his eyes had closed and he felt no desire to open them. Ally's sudden scream caused his head to jerk up, and his hand to drop to his gun.

"Don't move so much as an inch, lawman, or you'll be drawing that gun in Hell." Cooper's ugly face was within an inch of his. "Suddenly recalled where it was that I know you from. You were on a posse that tracked me an' a couple of other fellas after we pulled a bank job." His voice held a grim satisfaction that chilled Holland's blood. He laughed. "Good thing I keep a derringer hidden in my boot. Saw you nodding off and figured this would be the best chance to get the drop on you."

Ally screamed again. Horn was holding her as Sherwood ripped her shirt from her body, his fingers feeling for the buttons of her levis.

"Let's go join the party." Cooper prodded Holland with the derringer.

Stiffly, Holland got to his feet as

Ally gave another piercing scream. The shirt had been torn away, the levis were hanging open.

"Leave her alone, you bastards," shouted Holland, making to run for her, but Cooper put his hand in his chest to hold him back.

"I'll drill you, if you try anything," Cooper snarled.

The two men were holding Ally as best they could but she wasn't making it easy for them. The one hope that Holland had was the pistol that lay in the sand. None of them had bothered to pick it up, once they had disarmed Ally.

Cooper had moved to the front of Holland in order to get a good view of what was going on. Hurriedly, Holland glanced over his shoulder. Seizing what might be his first and last chance, he dived headlong at Cooper. The shot from the derringer went high and both men hit the ground. Ally, sensing her part in the attack, clung on to Horn and Sherwood.

Holland jumped to his feet and grabbed the fallen pistol. Spinning round, he shot Cooper through the head. Horn had disentangled himself from Ally and was reaching for Cooper's gun. Holland fired and shot him through the heart. Sherwood made a grab for Ally in an attempt to hold her in front of him as a shield, but Holland fired over Ally into Sherwood's head which burst like a melon. Sherwood spun backwards and hit the dirt, his eyes staring at the vultures that were already gathering.

The girl had collapsed on the ground, sobbing loudly, the check shirt in tatters. Taking a blanket from his saddle, Holland draped it round her shoulders. He helped her to the shade of a saguaro and laid her down. Then he put a canteen to her lips. At first she was reluctant to drink it, but his gentle persuasion got her to see sense.

He let the bodies lie where they had

fallen. "Even vultures deserve a meal," he said to her.

For a while they stayed where they were until Ally felt able to ride, then they moved on to Last Stop.

12

TO Morley standing in the batwings of the Lucky Lady, it seemed that the whole town was going to the Three Aces. Faulds had already gone down there. As a friend of the Lucky Lady's owner he had been invited to play in the big game, having the necessary capital to back his play.

Within a couple of hours, he thought, the saloon would be virtually empty and he could come back and take the loot out of the safe. By the time the game broke up, he'd be halfway to Casa Blanca, where he would meet Belle, then they'd go down to South America somewhere and open a real classy place with the money. It would be goodbye to Dak and Gant but, he reckoned, he could live with it.

Morley licked his lips at the thought of Belle and the money they'd have to open up a cat house on their own account.

"You ready?" Dak's voice startled him. He hadn't heard the giant mountain man coming up behind him.

"I'm ready," he said, pushing through the batwings and going out into the street.

They walked together to the Three Aces, which was already nearly full. Over the heads of the crowd he could see Faulds sitting at a table, puffing on a cheroot and talking to the saloon's owner and Lucas, the gambler who had put the idea into his head last night. There was another man at the table, a Negro dressed in a white silk shirt and silk cravat, a wide-brimmed hat by his elbow, a gold-topped cane resting against the edge of the table.

"Jack Lorrigan," Dak said, as though reading Morley's mind. "Hell of a card player."

"You don't say," replied Morley,

watching the Negro lounging back in his seat.

Morley and Dak pushed their way through to the bar and ordered a couple of beers.

Morley wondered how he could get rid of Dak. He did not want him hanging round half the night, he wanted to get over to the safe, empty it and then be on his way south.

They took their beers back to the table where the game was going to be played. They were in time to see Butler put a fresh pack on the table. Gant picked it up and broke the seal on it. Taking the cards out of the packet, he spread them fan-like across the table. Expertly, he gathered them up and started to deal, the blue-backed cards sliding across the green baize of the table. Morley watched as the players gathered the cards into their hands then sorted them out. Gant began the betting and the game got under way.

He watched for a while, then cast an eye about for Dak. He saw the burly man taking one of the dance-hall girls up the stairs. Morley waited until they had disappeared around the corner of the landing.

Edging through the crowd, Morley hesitated at the batwings, then gave a quick backward glance. The play was still going on; there was no sign of Dak or the girl on the stairs. He stepped out on to the sidewalk and quickly walked back towards the Lucky Lady.

The whole street was empty, so great was the attraction of the game at the Three Aces. No lights burned in the store or the café. Even the hitch rails were empty. The silence gave Morley the creeps as he walked down the street.

The entrance to the alley that ran down by the saloon gaped like a black hole as Morley got to it. He unhooked the leather thong over the hammer of his .45 and went down the alley. Halfway down he found the window. Morley took a knife from his pocket, opened the blade, then pushed it under the catch. A second later there was a click and Morley pushed up the window.

Reaching into his pocket he found a match, scraped it on his boot heel and climbed inside. Finding a lamp on Faulds' desk he lit it and its flame bathed the room in a weak yellow light. He moved the lamp from the desk and placed it on the safe. Slick fingers turned the combination, first to the right, then to the left, then the same again. The safe door clicked and opened.

Inside, he found the saddle-bags and with them a heap of greenbacks. He pulled out the saddle-bags and put them on the table behind him, then he took out the greenbacks and stuffed them in his pocket.

"Always figured you had your eye on them saddle-bags of loot." Dak had come in through the saloon, made his way silently down the corridor and opened the door without Morley hearing him.

Instinctively, Morley's hand fell to his gun butt.

"Hold it right there, you cheap chiseler," Dak said, seeing the movement in the light of the lamp as Morley leant over the desk.

Morley straightened up, keeping his hand away from his gun. "Was just comin' down for you. Thought it was time we headed out. Eli's lost his touch. Look at what he did for Wicks." He spoke quickly.

"Know what you'd've done for Eli an' me if I hadn't been suspicious of the way your eyes kept wondering over them saddle-bags," Dak said, his tone rising with anger.

"Gonna plug me?" Morley asked, watching Dak's gun hand.

"Maybe. It'd be a sight quicker an' not as painful for you than if I handed you over to Eli and Faulds," Dak spat out.

"Think of it, ol' pal," smarmed Morley pointing to the saddle-bags. "Think of all that stuff split two ways instead of three, an' all Faulds' stuff as well." He laughed and watched as Dak's eyes took in the stuff on the desk.

As they did so, Morley threw himself across the desk, barely missing the lamp. They hit the floor with a crash. Morley was trying to hold Dak's gun hand away, while Dak tried to gouge out his eyes with his free hand.

Morley forced Dak's hand away then bit deeply into the man's face. The unexpected tactic startled Dak so much he momentarily let go of Morley's eyes. Getting his hand into his pocket Morley pulled out the knife that he had used to break into the office, got the blade open and drove it down into Dak's throat. The blood spurted up, soaking Morley's face. The body twitched as Morley twisted the knife, then lay still. Morley reeled backwards, rubbing his pain-filled eye.

"Crazy bastard," he spat out, kicking at the motionless form. "You coulda been rich," he snarled, wiping the knife on the leg of his levis.

Grabbing the saddle-bags, he climbed out of the window and into the alley. The street was still silent, with no one about. Skirting the buildings, he made his way to the livery and saddled his horse. Even the liveryman was at the saloon watching the card game. In grim silence, the saddle-bags over his shoulder, his pockets stuffed with loot, he rode out of town, heading for Casa Blanca and Belle.

13

THE big poker game finished as dawn broke. The winner was Faulds. He came out of the saloon $10,000 ahead. The others were philosophical about their losses. They could afford to lose. It squeezed Gant, but did not unduly perturb him, not with all the other stuff in Faulds' safe.

He yawned and stretched his way through the batwings and out into the warm, fresh air of the early morning. Cigar smoke and the taste of whiskey were still in his throat.

As Faulds came out, Gant searched for Morley and Dak. It didn't worry him, not seeing them. He had seen the big man take a girl upstairs and figured he was still there with her. Morley, he guessed, had probably hit the sack, not being a card man. The way he was going on about that whore he had hidden away in Casa Blanca, he was more likely mooning over her.

Gant and Faulds crossed the rutted street and walked down to the Lucky Lady. Faulds unlocked the door and pushed it open. Before the game had started he had left word with Danny, his head barkeep, to lock up at twelve, no matter what, and leave the key for him in the Three Aces.

"Care for a glass, Eli?" he asked, as they went in. With $10,000 in his pocket he could afford to be generous with his best brandy.

"Don't mind if I do. Then I aim to get some sleep before tonight's session." Gant laughed as he wiped his hand across his mouth.

"You aim to make a killing?" Faulds led him down the passage to his office.

"Sure do," Gant bragged, feeling he could not have two nights of bad luck, even against the professional gamblers he had just been playing.

"What's the matter?" Gant saw the expression change on Faulds' face as they got to the office.

"Don't know, Eli. But something isn't right." As he opened the door, Faulds drew his gun. Gant followed suit.

"What the hell's happened?" demanded Faulds, seeing Dak's body and the opened safe — minus its contents. "Damn," he blazed. "Some thieving bastard has emptied me out."

Gant stared at Dak's body for a moment, then he looked over Faulds' shoulder. "Got my stash as well."

"Who'd have the face to do it?"

"I can guess who," Gant stormed.

Glancing away from the safe, Faulds let out a bull-like snort. "Who?"

"That double-crossing murderer, Morley. Who'd you think? Probably fixing to run out on me an' split the stuff with his whore. Damn his hide." His voice was scathing, cutting the air like a red-hot knife.

"Damn him," cursed Faulds. "Where the hell's he gone?"

"Gone to see that little whore, Belle,"

fumed Gant, beating the table with his balled fist, his mean face a mask of rage.

"We're gonna have to get after him." Faulds checked the loads in his pistol. "I've got a few good men. We can catch up with him in no time at all."

"No," roared Gant, whose anger showed no signs of abating. "He's mine. I'm gonna catch up with him and cut him into a million little pieces."

"Save a lump for me to hack on." Faulds bent down to examine the safe once more.

"You'd best be quick," Gant told him as he went through the door.

He ran outside and went directly to the livery.

"I need a horse an' I need it now," he yelled at the old liveryman, who had banked on getting a couple of hours sleep now that the big game had finished. One thing he didn't need was a loco man storming in and demanding a horse there and then.

Scratching his balding head, he threw

a truculent scowl at Gant. "Just hang on a minute. I got a horse, but you're gonna have to pay for him," he shouted at the outlaw.

Gant, who was boiling with rage, drew his Colt and flourished it under the liveryman's face. "This payment enough?" he demanded, pulling back the hammer.

The liveryman gulped loudly; he was old, and life held few further pleasures for him, but he was in no rush to meet his Maker.

"Y-yessir," he gabbled, spittle flooding out of his toothless mouth.

"Saddle him up." Gant uncocked the gun and put it back in its holster. The old fool wouldn't give him any trouble.

A few minutes later, the liveryman led a mare from its stall and saddled her, all the time watching Gant stamping up and down the stable, fit to bust. Wondering if Gant's temper would snap before he got the horse ready, after what seemed an age of fiddling about, he called over, "Ready mister."

Spitting out the piece of straw that he had been massacring with his teeth, Gant swung up into the saddle.

The liveryman gulped. "You gonna pay for that cayuse?"

"See Faulds; he'll pay you for it." Rowelling the horse, he rode out of the stable, leaving the liveryman thankful to be alive, but wondering if he was going to get any money for the horse.

All the way out of town Gant cursed Morley for a thieving, no-good snake, a double-crosser and a murderer. He had been riding at a fair clip for about half an hour when he simmered down a bit and decided that with Dak dead, Wicks dead and Morley soon to join them he would need to do some rethinking. Once he got his stuff back from Morley he'd head back north and form a new gang. There was no shortage of men who would ride with him. He had a name for pulling off bank jobs and stage heists. He'd have no trouble at all. Then he'd paint the territory red — in somebody's blood. He licked his thin lips at the prospect, but first there was Morley to settle with.

Then, unaccountably his thoughts turned to Red Bluff and Jack Holland. Holland still had a posse out looking for them but, what the hell, he'd dodged posses before and would do so again. Red Bluff was behind him now. Holland, damn him to hell, was probably hunting the other end of the territory, if he was still hunting. And if he ran across him, well and good. He'd bite on a bullet. Straightening his back and focusing his thoughts on Morley and Casa Blanca he rowelled his horse and went a little faster.

* * *

Zeke Morley had no illusions as he approached the outskirts of the little border town of Casa Blanca. Gant would be storming mad once he discovered Dak's body beside the empty safe. He'd be sweating blood. But Morley didn't mind. One thing he'd learned was that an angry man doesn't fight that well. It was better to be cold, standing outside it all and let the other man do the worrying.

He'd known Eli long enough to realize that, despite his sly ways, his temper would often get the better of him. Perhaps that's why things had turned out the way they had. There should have been no going back to Red Bluff, Mordecai or no Mordecai. They'd tangled with a wild cat when they'd tangled with Holland and that town.

When Casa Blanca came into view from the top of a low rise Morley halted his horse briefly and looked down. Just a collection of adobe buildings, nothing much, but with a big white house in the town square, a house that had once been the hacienda of a wealthy Spaniard, then owned by a Mexican who presumed to become president, until a government firing squad put an end to his presumption. Now it was a cat house, the best damn cat house in the territory, and Belle its best damn whore. Soon, he thought, she'd be the richest whore in the place, and then they'd have the best cat house in South America. He sleeved his face and pushed his horse down the shallow slope towards Casa Blanca.

Morley rode through the gates of the hacienda into the cool courtyard, shaded by trees. The door of the cat house opened and Slocum came to the door. Slocum was one of the house mincers, a burly black man of six foot six. His body strained at the seams of his shirt and waistcoat. Recognizing Morley he came down the steps, his hand raised in welcome.

"Good to see you, Zeke," he said taking the leathers of Morley's horse and hitching it to the rail when Morley got down.

"Hi, Slocum, you old horse thief," Morley grinned, taking the other man's hand. "Belle up and about?"

"Belle's still working. Big rancher's been entertaining a few friends. Kept the girls at it all night. They're not bothered though. It's more *dinero* for them." A loud laugh came from the barrel-chested man.

"Can you fix me up with a room where I can grab a few hours shut eye?" Morley gave Slocum a knowing look which Slocum interpreted instantly:

"You running from the law again?" he asked.

"It's more serious than that. Ol' Gant's double-crossed me. Killed Dak and Wicks. Figgerin' to finish me off next," Morley lied.

Raising an eyebrow, Slocum said, "Right sad to hear that, Zeke. Never know when you can trust a man an' when you can't."

Slocum led Morley round the back of the cat house to something that was no better than a shed where they threw the customers when they got a bit unruly, so they could sleep off the drink without going home to disturb their wives. The place was dark and smelly, but it had an iron bed and clean sheets.

"Sure appreciate this, Slocum, my friend. Make it up to you one day soon."

"No need for that. It's my pleasure." With that Slocum went out and Morley lay down, but not before putting his gun within easy reach. Then, he fell asleep.

14

FAULDS didn't like the look of Holland from the moment he came into his saloon with the girl in tow. Trouble hovered over their heads like a hungry vulture. Faulds had been about to round up his men and catch up with Gant in case Eli had any ideas about taking off with his stash of greenbacks as well, but something about the way Holland looked when he walked in through the batwings stopped him dead.

Holland leaned against the bar with Ally behind him and ordered two beers from the barkeep. Faulds waved Danny away and served them himself. Holland and Ally were taking a good gander around the place.

"Tryin' to find somebody, fella?" Faulds asked, as he pulled the beers.

"A couple of friends of mine. They

might have passed this way." Holland went on to give Faulds a fair description of Gant and Dak and Morley.

Faulds watched Holland as he spoke. Lawman, for sure, he thought.

"If they're friends of yours I'm the next President," he told Holland with a sneer.

"My name's Jack Holland. Used to be sheriff of Red Bluff. And I want them all real bad. Real bad." He spoke sharply, causing a few heads along the bar to turn his way.

Faulds considered the matter for a moment. If he caught up with Morley there'd be killing. Either way it could be to his advantage.

"They've both been through. Headin' for Casa Blanca. It's just south of here. Mean set of *hombres*, but then I guess you know that. They ain't been gone all that long either."

Holland watched Faulds over the rim of his glass. The man was telling the truth, but he was holding something back.

"I'll be on my way then." Draining the glass, Holland felt Ally's hand on his shoulder.

"We'll be on our way," she said as he turned to face her. He saw the look of determination in her face.

"You can't come. It's not going to be a job for a woman."

"Well, you ain't leaving me here. If you did it would be like leaving me with Blair. And you're not doing that." Her voice was grim like she meant it.

From the look in her face, Holland knew that it would be pointless arguing with her. It would just be wasting valuable time.

"OK, let's go."

As they pushed their way through the batwings, Faulds gave the barkeep the come on.

"Git the boys and make it quick. We're going after those two," he whispered.

Faulds plan was simplicity itself. He was going to let Holland and the girl catch up with Gant and Morley and then let the three of them settle things between them. Then he'd step in and pick up the pieces.

Dak's blood still stained the floor when Faulds told the three gunmen about it.

* * *

Morley woke about midday. Getting out of bed he made his way round to the back of the cat house where he found Slocum in the kitchen preparing food for the girls.

"Got some for me?" His voice held a friendly tone as he went into the kitchen.

"Sure have." Slocum forked a couple of pieces of bacon out of the frying pan and on to the plate that Morley was holding.

"Now, if you'll just wait here, I'll get Belle for you." He disappeared through the swing door into the parlour where the girls waited for the customers. Moments later, as he was slicing up the bacon, Morley heard the delighted screech of Belle as Slocum told her that he had arrived.

She came through the door like a tornado, her arms outstretched ready to receive his embrace. Morley stood up and quickly swallowed the bacon, then flung out his arms to hug her. His grease-covered lips covered her mouth and his hands ran over her slim body.

Belle Gray was a small, golden-haired girl whose looks had not yet succumbed to the climate of Arizona or showed the ravages of her profession.

"It's good to see you, Zeke," she gasped when she had broken away from his suffocating embrace.

"An' it's good to see you, Belle," he told her. "We're rich." He pointed to the saddle-bags on the table.

"You got it off the ol' buzzard," she chortled like a little bird.

"Yeah, an' it wasn't no big deal, either. Slick as a whistle," he bragged, giving her another squeeze.

Belle's face rumpled into a frown. "What about Dak, an' Wicks?" she asked.

Morley let go of her and cut himself another piece of bacon. "Wicks collected a bullet in the belly at some no-account town. An' Dak's dead. Had to spear him to git the money."

Belle laughed and danced around the kitchen, an ecstatic expression on her face. "South America, here we come." She looked round in disgust. "An' goodbye to this dump."

Morley cleaned up the plate with a piece of bread, then finished his coffee and stood up. "Now let's go upstairs an' you can show me your new tricks."

Belle giggled as he took her hand and led her out of the kitchen. "The first thing you can do it get a bath an' a shave. A drummer came in an' gave me some French perfume. You can tip it in the bath water. Might make you smell better. Then we'd better get out of this hole before Gant gets down here."

"Don't worry about Eli, he'll be playin' poker for days."

* * *

Gant pushed his horse real hard under the desert sun, so hard that white lather soon broke out on its coat. His spurs punished its flanks until they bled. His red-hot anger was slow to abate and was then replaced by a cold rage. Morley wasn't going to get away with it, even if he had to chase him to Hell. He passed saguaro cacti, with their thick arms filled with spines, fantastic rock formations, all without really seeing them, so fixed was his mind on Morley and what he would do to him. As the day passed so did the miles and soon he found himself on the outskirts of Casa Blanca.

Dismounting, Gant found the livery stable.

"You got a fresh horse to trade for this one?" he asked the liveryman.

"*Si, señor.*" The plump Mexican

scratched his body as he gave Gant's horse the once over.

"OK," Gant told him. "Saddle him up for me. An' be quick about it."

The Mexican jumped at the barked tone of Gant's voice and scurried inside to do his bidding. While he waited Gant stood at the end of the street. There were very few people about in the vicinity of Casa Blanca. As he thought about the cat house he worked out a plan. Morley would be expecting him, he told himself, but he would not expect him to come barrelling in through the front door and up the stairs which is where he probably was with Belle.

"Your horse, *señor*," a voice said from behind him.

The shock was so unexpected that Gant had his pistol out of his holster before he could think.

"Please," quivered the man. "Do not kill me." He handed Gant the reins of the horse. Putting his gun away, Gant ran his eyes over the horse.

"OK," he laughed. "Not this time. Next time — maybe." Taking the reins from the Mexican, he led the horse in the direction of the cat house.

At the hitch rail outside the house, he tied the horse then rolled himself a stogie. Before starting up the path, he struck a match on the heel of his boot. It flared briefly, then he threw it away and started up the path.

The lights were on in the downstairs rooms and the sound of piano music drifted out through the window. Checking his pistols, Gant mounted the steps. A drunken cowboy lurched out of the front door, light flooding the path. His smile froze when he saw the murderous intent in Gant's eyes; the colour draining from his face, he lurched off down the path and into the street.

Gant went inside. Two cowboys were sitting on chairs waiting for girls. Ignoring them, Gant went towards the stairs and made to go up. One of the cowboys got up to bar Gant's way.

"We were here first, fella." His face was red with anger and lust.

For an answer Gant drew his gun and shot him in the chest. The cowboy staggered back, blood squirting from his chest, his gun undrawn. His companion jumped to his feet, his hand reaching for his .45, but Gant cut him down before he could clear leather.

Slocum was in the kitchen getting himself a snack during a break in the evening's entertainment. Grabbing the shot-gun propped against the table, he ran into the hall in time to see Gant going up the stairs. Before he could really take in the carnage before him, Gant had spun and put two slugs into his chest. He fell backwards, firing both barrels into the ceiling.

Doors were opening all over the cat house as worried customers came out to see if their spouse had caught up with them; whores screamed and covered themselves with a variety of garments, including a Roman toga. Seeing Gant with a smoking gun in his hand they immediately went back inside.

Knowing where Belle's room lay, Gant ran down the corridor, kicked the door open and found Morley asleep in a drunken stupor. He shook him until some life started to return to the inert body.

When the eyes slowly flickered open Gant put his gun away and took Morley by the hair. Dragging him up until he was in a sitting position, he started to lash him with his open hand, until Morley's head went from side to side, leaving the dazed outlaw just about conscious.

"Come on, where is it?" demanded Gant.

"Wha — what?" gulped Morley who was still not sure what was happening.

"My money, that's what." Gant's hand went to work again on Morley's face so that a patch of red covered it from cheek to cheek as he slapped it from side to side.

"Eli, for Christ's sake, don't kill me.

It's in the wardrobe in the next room." Morley pointed to the adjoining door.

Gant flung Morley back against the pillows and strode across the room. "Now you stay there, Morley, or I'll put one in you." Something he planned on doing anyway.

Wrenching open the door Gant went inside to see a tall wardrobe standing against the wall. In it was a heap of clothes. Gant dragged them out, throwing them anywhere. At the bottom of the heap were the saddle-bags that contained the stash. He smiled to himself and threw the bags over his shoulder. In the next room he heard the telltale creak of floorboards.

As he went through the door he saw that the bed was empty.

"It ain't over yet, Gant," Morley was standing in the middle of the room, a gun in his hand, his eyes riveted on Gant, his mind full of hatred for his former pard.

Gant hardly hesitated. His gun came into his hand, the shot exploded and with it Morley's chest. His knees sagged and his gun fell from his grasp. Striding over to the corpse, Gant spat at it, his smoking gun still in his hand.

"You bastard," screamed Belle from the doorway, her hair wild like her eyes.

Ignoring her, Gant went to the table at the side of the bed, and picked up the whiskey bottle. Spitting out the cork he tilted his head back and took a long swallow. Belle knelt at Morley's side, crying quietly. Putting the bottle down, Gant picked her up and threw her on the bed. The transparent shift came open revealing her pink breasts. Pinning her to the bed Gant opened his levis as her screams became hysterical.

15

HOLLAND rode into Casa Blanca just ahead of Ally. As he turned into the main street where the cat house stood, he saw the crowd gathered round the place.

"Could be we're too late and Gant's been and gone," he said to Ally.

"Just what I was thinking. Then again, maybe Gant's still here." She pulled up her horse alongside Holland. "That crowd's got to be staring at something. Perhaps Gant's still in there with a bullet in him."

Shaking his head slowly, Holland said, "Somehow I don't think so." His hand clenched round the leathers of the bay, "I want Gant to still be alive, I want to put him under myself or see him hang." The hatred in Holland's eyes burned like a fire.

"Let's get down there and find out

what's happened. You take the horses down to the livery and get them fed and watered, I'll go and ask around." The bay needed little urging, sensing water and rest.

Dismounting while Ally went to find the livery stable Holland walked towards the crowd.

He tapped a fella in a stovepipe hat and brown city-bought suit on the shoulder.

"Good day, sir," the brown stovepipe said, facing Holland, puffing up his chest as he put his thumbs in his lapels, "I'm Jedediah Cornwall, drummer by occupation, actor by inclination," the drummer said, with a flourish of his stovepipe and bowing low.

Holland smiled at the man. It takes all sorts, he thought. "Well, perhaps you can tell me what's been going on here." Holland nodded in the direction of the white building.

"A most grisly affair," began Jedediah Cornwall. "A mass shooting. Notorious outlaw by the name of Eli Gant butchered a score or more people in there. Blood and bodies everywhere." His voice rang out like an actor's delivering a dramatic speech with all the gestures to go with it.

"What about Gant himself?" Holland asked, with a trace of impatience at Jedediah's unnecessary elaboration of the story.

"Fled into the desert, I know not where," Jedediah concluded. Then, he suddenly pointed in the direction of a bulky figure who was approaching the throng. Holland could see the star shining on his vest. Leaving Jedediah declaiming he approached the sheriff.

"Just a minute, Sheriff," Holland said quickly, sensing the man was the self-important type, not inclined to listen to strangers, let alone a stranger who had come into town just when something big had broken out and required all the sheriff's attention.

The fat, puffy-faced sheriff heaved to a stop as did those behind him. Although he wore two tied-down Colts,

Holland doubted if he could use them effectively. In fact, from the way he was puffing, Holland didn't think he could get them out of their holsters.

"What is it? What is it?" he demanded, importantly. "Can't you see I'm busy? Worst shooting in the history of the West."

"The drummer just told me." Try as he might Holland was having real trouble holding his temper in check. In his years as a lawman, he had encountered sheriffs like the one before him, and in his opinion they did more harm than good.

"Now just hold your mouth. Can't say I like your tone of voice. Nobody talks to Sheriff Billy Higgs like that." He puffed himself up so much that Holland saw his trousers slip and inch over his fat gut.

"This is urgent," he snapped. Every minute he stood arguing in the street with the fat turkey in front of him Gant was getting that much further away.

"So is what's gone on in the cat

house." Sheriff Billy Higg's jowls bumped up and down as he spoke. "And it's something I've got to sort out," he snorted at Holland.

Finally losing patience, Holland drew his gun and stuck it under Sheriff Billy Higgs's nose. "Now, you tell me who's in that cat house and if Gant ain't in there, you can tell me where he might be."

The crowd had fallen silent as Holland spoke. Sheriff Billy Higgs's face turned a deep purple and he seemed to be struggling for breath. The sweat ran down his forehead; his little round eyes seemed to grow out of his head.

"Gant ain't in there. He's hightailed it. Killed Belle an' her lover as well as Slocum an' another couple of fellas." His voice quivered shakily as he spoke.

"Any idea where Gant's gone?" Holland demanded, reinforcing the question by pushing his gun into the sheriff's ribs.

"If he's any sense, he'll get over the

border. He'll have to stop at Ghost Creek first for some water." He gabbled so fast that Holland had some difficulty making sense of what he said, but he got the gist of it.

"Where's Ghost Creek?" he asked. The crowd were starting to get restless, and Holland wondered how long it would be before one of them tried to jump him. He hoped they wouldn't, he didn't want to shoot any innocent party on Gant's account. His quarrel was with Gant.

The sweat running freely down his face, Higgs said, in a barely audible voice. "Half a day's ride south."

Holland put away his gun. "I'm going after Gant. You can follow if you want to, but he's mine."

Sheriff Billy Higgs's face showed a deal of relief, and Holland guessed that it meant that the sheriff would not be raising a posse. He did not know what the sheriff would tell the townsfolk, and he did not care either. He had the feeling that any posse led by Higgs would just get in the way.

He found Ally at the livery stable, the horses fed and watered.

"Where do you think you're going?" he asked, climbing up into the saddle.

"I'm going with you after Gant," she told him in a voice that would not be contradicted.

"No, you aren't," Holland told her, laying his hand on the leathers of her horse.

"Sorry, Holland, we've come this far together, we might as well go the rest of the way. Besides I feel as though I owe a favour. You did get me out of that mess with Horn and the others."

With a deeply resigned shrug, he said, "OK." They soon left Casa Blanca behind them.

* * *

Out in the desert among the weirdly sculpted rocks and the saguaro with their spines and fat, arm-like features and grey-green colour, Eli Gant felt good. The full saddle-bags lay across the back of his horse. Morley lay dead in the cat house along with that no-good Belle. His canteen was full of fresh water and his horse fed and rested. The border lay a day's ride away. This time tomorrow, he thought, I'll be spending money and having the best whores that *dinero* can buy, along with the best food in this part of the world. He laughed to himself as he rode on.

The first thing to do was to head for Ghost Creek. The place had been deserted since the silver ran out. Gant remembered it from the old days. Once upon a time, the citizens' committee had run him and the others out of the town and told them to stay out. Once more he laughed at the poetic justice of it. Coming back in a lonely triumph, so to speak, his pockets filled with gold. Damn shame there was nobody there to see him. They could have put on a band for him and had a picnic.

* * *

Faulds had three men with him and they were heading for Casa Blanca. The more Faulds thought about it, the more he knew that leaving Gant to Holland might not be such a good idea. Holland looked as though he could handle himself. He might be caught up in a very complicated situation. What made it worse was that he had been told that Apaches had been seen roaming about in the vicinity of Ghost Creek. That meant they would be heading towards Last Stop, looking to pick up some horses or some women from the outlying settlers. They might even take it into their heads to attack Casa Blanca itself. If they did that he would run headlong into them. He swore, damning Morley and damning Gant.

* * *

Gant reached Ghost Creek in the late afternoon. The buildings were still there clustered round the old well. The place had an eerie quality about it, with a breeze blowing dust and sagebrush through it. At the edge of the deserted town, Gant halted his horse and slipped the leather thong over the hammer of his six gun. Then he pushed on towards the well. Other than the creaking of a few shutters that had half blown off their hinges and were slamming against the wall, the place was silent.

Dismounting, he unlooped his canteen, and put it to his lips and drained the last few drops from it. He'd really gone through the water since leaving Casa Blanca. Then he let it fall to the ground. Drawing his gun he turned and fired. The Apache took the slug full in the chest. It sent him spinning backwards, blood exploding out of his shattered chest cavity.

Two came in quick succession. Gant fired twice, cutting them both down, their screams dying on their lips. His horse turned and trotted away from the gunfire. Gant made to run after it, but a slug tore into the dust at his feet. He went to the ground and put two slugs through the window of the hotel which he guessed they were using for cover.

Breaking open the loading gates, Gant flung the spent cartridge shells away and reloaded the pistol. Cautiously he looked up in the direction of the derelict hotel. He could see no sign of any movement. Then he saw a flicker as a shape passed the window. A second later a shell cut into the ground in front of his face. That settled it as far as Gant was concerned, he jumped to his feet and ran behind the well, which gave him better cover.

The light was starting to fail and Gant knew that once it went he was done for: they'd sneak up in the dark and cut his throat or maybe worse. Behind him was a store or what had once been a store. Once in there he felt he might have a better chance of standing them off — at least until morning. His horse was about twenty yards away, pawing at the ground.

There wasn't a chance of getting to him. But if the cayuse stayed where he was he might be able to get to him in the dark. Besides it had the saddle-bags on its back.

He gauged the distance. The Apaches weren't the best shots in the world, so maybe he'd make it. Zig-zagging he sprinted for the store, shots kicking up dust all around him. Shoulder charging the door he tumbled inside, chips of wood flying off the frame. Running to the window, he smashed it with the butt of his gun. Two Apaches were crossing the square as bullets flew against the side of the store, as other Apaches covered them. Gant fired twice, but did not hit either of them. The two Apaches dropped behind the well and started to fire at him. Suddenly, they got up and rushed towards the store. Gant drew a bead on one and squeezed the trigger. The Apache threw up his arms and tumbled backwards. Before Gant could shoot the second charging Apache, a rifle shot rang out and he too fell into the dust.

"I'll be damned," muttered Gant as a fresh burst of fire slammed into the store. Somebody, positioned in a line with the hotel, was pouring fire into it. Suddenly, the Apaches had had enough; from the cover of the hotel they ran into the street and vaulted on to their horses and rode off in a storm of dust and gunfire.

"Yeah," Gant laughed as the last of the Apaches disappeared down the street. The sudden relief that flowed through him made him miss the figure of Jack Holland as he appeared from the side of the house he had been using for cover.

As he walked into the street Gant's face dropped and a cold feeling gripped his heart.

"Gant," shouted Holland as he walked towards his quarry.

"You picked a fine place to die, Holland," Gant called back as they edged closer to each other.

They were within ten feet of each

other when Gant went for his gun. Twice Holland's gun blazed out. Gant sprawled in the dust. For a moment Holland stood motionless in the middle of the street then put his gun away.

"Nice shooting, Sheriff. Or should I say ex-Sheriff. Turn round, real slow." Holland recognized Faulds' voice.

When he turned he saw Ally whom he had left in the safety of the rocks, being held by one of Faulds' men with a gun at her head.

"Can't rightly call it a stand off, seeing as how I've got all the aces," Faulds said as he walked over to Gant's horse and retrieved the saddle-bags.

"If you plan on killing me," Holland asked him, "at least let the girl go."

Tossing the saddle-bags over his shoulder, Faulds said, "I hadn't planned on killing anybody — except Eli. And since you've saved me the trouble I can't see that we have any further business." He nodded to one of his henchmen. "Let the girl go."

The man pushed Ally towards Holland.

"Can't see as how there's any love lost between you and the folks of Red Bluff after what she told me. An' all I want is my money, which I got." He tapped the saddle-bags. "And Eli's loot for the trouble he put me to."

Holland could find no fault with that. He certainly wasn't inclined to argue the point. Faulds touched the brim of his hat in salute and mounted up followed by his men.

Putting his arm round Ally's shoulder, Holland felt the beginnings of a new life with Ally stir in him.

THE END

Other titles in the
Linford Western Library:

TOP HAND
Wade Everett

The Broken T was big. But no ranch is big enough to let a man hide from himself.

GUN WOLVES OF LOBO BASIN
Lee Floren

The Feud was a blood debt. When Smoke Talbot found the outlaws who gunned down his folks he aimed to nail their hide to the barn door.

SHOTGUN SHARKEY
Marshall Grover

The westbound coach carrying the indomitable Larry and Stretch headed for a shooting showdown.